Discovering Us

True Love Trilogy #1

Harper Bentley

To Christi
Much love!
Harper Bentley

Dedication

To Melissa for always making me feel like I can do anything

Acknowledgements

You know who you are. You're the ones who constantly encourage me, pick me up when I'm down, and give me your unfailing love and support always. And for that, I love you. Thank you for being so damned awesome.

Prologue

They say nothing improves the memory more than trying to forget.

Well, this "They" can bite me.

As far as I'm concerned, the hippocampus in my brain which stores long-term memory (yeah, I've looked that shit up) can go screw itself. And since I'm going there, the prefrontal cortex can take a hike too. If it wasn't for my stupid cranium, I think my mental health would be just fine, thank you very much. And that's not a weirdly ironic statement, huh? But as it stands, my awesome retention of past happenings has played just too strong a role in my life leading me to some serious heartache.

I'm twenty-five years old, I've had a mostly decent life so far, but when the memories invade my mind… they always lead me back to Jag.

And I become a mess.

See, Jagger Knox Jensen was already set up for stardom with a cooler-than-hell name (his father had played lead guitar in a pretty famous rock band in the 70s and decided that any kids of his needed awesome names to go with the "cool" that came with, well, playing in a pretty famous rock band in the 70s).

Then there was me, set on the path to the humdrums with my very plain, very average name. Um, thanks again, Mom, for naming me after that Ripley chick in those *Alien* movies. Appreciate it. No, really.

My name is Ellen Love. Bleh. Saying my name aloud sounds like you're trying to tell someone what letter's in my last name. Insert look of disgust here.

Anyway, growing up, Jag and I lived on the same block in a suburb just outside of Chicago. I was a certified tomboy (having three older brothers I really had no other choice), and since Jag and I were the only kids around the same age in our neighborhood, we played together almost every day for years.

Summers found us riding our bikes up and down our tree-lined street, swimming in the heated pool in my backyard, or writing our names with silvery sparklers on the Fourth of July; winters we'd plop onto our backs to make snow angels in each other's powdery-white-blanketed front yards, drink hot chocolate loaded with melty marshmallows in the clubhouse in his backyard, or run to each other's houses hauling along what wonderful wealth of goodies Santa had brought us.

The entwinement of our lives was fated from the moment the ice cream truck slowly meandered its way through the neighborhood, and as we both eagerly licked on our Spiderman pops, we realized we were the only kids our age in the area.

And thus our story began.

This is the first part of it. Bear with me. There's been a lot of shit that's gone down.

Chapter 1

I was five when I first kissed Jag.

I'll never forget it. Ever.

Jag's older by ten years sister Starr—see? Cool rock star kid name—had taken us to see *Beauty and the Beast* the weekend before and we'd both been awed that when Beast had kissed Belle at the end, a profusion of sparkles had shot up around them into a display of fireworks and then the ugly gargoyles on his castle turned to radiant angels. How freaking cool was *that*? So the next school day when we were at recess on the playground (Jag was on the big-kid side of the fence since he was a second grader and I was trapped in kindergarten-land), he came to the chain link fence that separated us and hollered out, "El, come here!" In my little girls' red, pleated coat and black Mary Janes (Mom was still trying to turn me into a girl) I ran over to see what he wanted. His glacier blue eyes great big in his little boy face danced when he shouted, "Let's see if it works!" Then he stuck his lips through the links all pursed and ready to be smacked. Without a second thought, I leaned in and landed a big one on him. We pulled back and looked around, a little disappointed that there was no sparkle, no fireworks, no changing of statues from evil to good (there were no statues around but we thought maybe some of the mean teachers could've been transformed… it was worth a shot), but then we both giggled and he ran away, swiping at that one hunk of his dark hair that always fell into his eyes, telling me over his shoulder that he'd see me after school.

I didn't know then that that particular scene, his running from me, would play out again in our lives as I stood laughing after him.

Well, I'm definitely not laughing now.

Chapter 2

I was ten when I fell in love with Jag.

We were on the bus riding home from school when Kyle Wade decided he wanted the Giordano's gift card I'd won in math class that day. Kyle was a huge kid—he was supposed to be in Jag's class but he'd flunked a couple times—and the class bully. He'd gotten in my face telling me I was a dumbass, which had earned a gasp from me since I wasn't used to that kind of language from kids our age, then he'd grabbed my backpack, digging through it to pilfer the card. Of course, since I wasn't a sissy by any means, I'd stood up to him, grabbing my bag back indignantly which was when he hauled off and punched me in the face, breaking my nose. Um, who knew pizza meant that much to the kid? Jeez.

I dropped back down into my bus seat stunned, while my best friend Rebecca Stark who sat with me freaked out as she dug to find a tissue in her bag as the blood from my nose continued to drip onto my Ace of Base (yeah, I know) t-shirt. We watched as Kyle proceeded to dig diligently through my bag, haphazardly tossing everything out into the aisle. That was until he suddenly went flying, landing face first on the bus floor with a loud "Oomph!" I watched in amazement as Jag pinned him there, his knee digging into Kyle's back, and he whispered in the kid's ear that if he touched me again, he'd kill him. Wow.

After Jag jerked Kyle up off the floor by his shirt collar—the kid was now snot bawling which almost made me feel sorry for him… almost—Jag made him pick everything up and put it back in my bag, hand it back to me nicely, and apologize. When he was satisfied, Jag reminded Kyle of his previous warning then Jag punched him good and hard in the stomach as he sat him in a bus seat, telling him he'd better stop crying or he and his friends would mess him up but good.

Jag's blue eyes glittered wildly as he smiled at me while he pushed that shock of dark hair out of his face, asking, "That good enough, El?"

All I could do was nod at him in admiration then he went to the back of the bus to sit with his buddies once again.

Rebecca looked at me, her brown eyes huge. "That was awesome," she whispered.

"Yeah," I said all nasally, holding the tissue to my nose.

Great. Mom was going to kill me for getting blood on my shirt. But God knew she loved her Spray 'N Wash. With my three older brothers practically rolling in dirt all day long, the woman literally had a black belt in cleaning, so her eyes would probably glaze over in lust at the opportunity of scrubbing my shirt into submission, getting it back to looking like new.

But when I got home, lo and behold, my sanguine-stained shirt wasn't even an issue as my mother whisked me off to the emergency room to have my nose reset. And a great, big YEOWWCH on that one. When I got home, I looked in the mirror and let out a groan when I saw two black eyes glaring back at me like two multicolored beacons of pain behind the bandage that covered my nose. Pretty. But my brothers had thought I was "The Shit," which garnered them a dirty look from Mom, and their approval through giving me soft arm punches made me happy, so it was all good.

Since Dad was an attorney, he'd contacted Kyle's parents to let them know what'd happened, and after they told Dad they'd cover all medical costs, he let them off the hook, an apology being all he was after, well, that and a promise that they'd look into their son's bullying problem.

Dad had also wanted to contact the school about Mr. Abernathy, the bus driver, but I talked him out of it. He'd asked me why he hadn't stopped the bus when Kyle had started his crap. Well, Mr. A was hard of hearing and when one of the littler kids had told him what'd happened (after he'd dropped off Kyle), Mr. A had felt horrible and had apologized about a kabillion times to me for not stopping and taking care of things. He said his hearing aid batteries had gone out that afternoon and he hadn't had time to replace them, so he hadn't heard what was going on. And since his hearing was impaired, he'd had to really pay attention to traffic; therefore, he hadn't seen what had occurred in the bus mirror. But he was a sweet old man who'd lost his wife two years before and I told Dad that he was a good driver, he was nice to all us kids, and that if he'd heard what was going on, he would've stopped. So taking that all into consideration, Dad didn't call, thank goodness.

The best part of the whole situation? Jag had thought I looked cool and badass with two black eyes and I didn't think I could love him any more.

Chapter 3

I was still ten when I knew I was going to marry Jag.

That summer, my brother Robbie had just turned sixteen. The next weekend he and my other brothers Mike and Jake—Mom was at least consistent in her love for plain names—who were seventeen and nineteen, respectively, had been at the lake, and I mean, THE lake, Lake Michigan, with a bunch of friends. They'd rented Jet Skis and had gone out that morning. But by that afternoon, we didn't know if Robbie was going to live. He'd had an accident when he and another of the boys had collided on their watercrafts.

Mom, Dad and I had rushed frantically to the hospital when Jake had called. By the time we got there, Robbie was already in surgery for a ruptured spleen. My Dad was livid, screaming at Jake that Robbie wasn't old enough to be riding alone and that Jake should've been more responsible. Jake was already crying his eyes out, so the accusation hadn't helped much. What made it worse was when Dad then grabbed and hugged Jake tightly as they cried in each other's arms. I was horrified watching my family this way. I'd never seen my dad cry. Heck, I'd never seen my brothers cry, so my world was turned upside down as I stood there trying to comprehend all that was going on around me.

I don't know when he showed up, but at some point when I'd been sitting in one of those hard, plastic, connected-to-five-other-chairs chairs in the waiting room, I realized Jag was sitting beside me, and he was holding my hand. I looked down to where we were connected just staring for the longest time, not able to tell which fingers were whose after a bit. When I finally looked up, Jag just smiled softly and gave me a little nod.

And that was when I knew. I knew I was going to marry Jagger Knox Jensen.

We stayed that way for a long time with neither of us speaking. We stayed that way until the doctor came out and told Mom and Dad that Robbie was going to be okay, it'd just take some time for him to heal. The relief was palpable in the room and different kinds of tears flowed then as everybody hugged.

"Thank you," I whispered to Jag through my tears as I looked into his startling blue eyes.

He squeezed my hand in answer then continued sitting beside me for what seemed like hours, both of us still silent. The next thing I remembered was being put into my bed by my dad.

"Is Robbie home?" I asked sleepily.

"No, honey. He'll be in the hospital for a while, but he'll be home soon. You go back to sleep. Mom will be here with you." He kissed my forehead and left the room to go back to stay with and keep watch over his youngest son.

I was still awake when Mom came in to check on me. "Is Robbie okay?" I asked.

"Yes, baby. We're very lucky." She tucked my soft comforter under my chin.

"How did Jag get there?"

"His parents came as soon as they heard. When they were leaving, Jag refused to leave you. I told them we'd take him home. He never left your side," she said with a smile, sweeping the hair back off my forehead as she bent to kiss me there.

"He's a good guy," I muttered sleepily.

"Yes, he certainly is." She kissed my forehead again then left my room as I drifted off.

Jag was there the next morning when I came downstairs for breakfast, checking to make sure I was okay. He stayed and played video games with me to keep my mind off things, I figured out later, then went with us to the hospital to see Robbie.

That was the scariest time in my life up to that point, but Jag was there throughout it all. And I knew. *Knew* we'd be together forever.

Chapter 4

I was eleven when Jag broke my heart for the first time.

"Oh, man! That's the coolest skateboard I've ever seen!" Jag said in admiration, turning the page back in the magazine he was looking at and shoving it in my face, showing it to me.

"That *is* pretty cool," I replied.

We were sitting on the front steps of my house drinking root beer floats, our favorite, and taking a break from skating. Jag had shown me earlier how to do a nollie kickflip and I'd been working on it for an hour in the driveway but not quite getting it right. I'd gotten frustrated, but I had to give it to him. He had an infinite amount of patience when it came to teaching me board tricks. Well, if you tuned out his yelling at me to stop being such a girl and do it right.

After that day, I'd saved for the next eight months to buy the skateboard for his thirteenth birthday, putting away my own birthday, Christmas, and allowance money to make his dream come true.

On the day of his party, I was so excited to give him his present I could hardly stand it. The skateboard had come in the week before and I'd wrapped it immediately after the postman had handed it over. I just knew Jag would love it. I'd hinted to him, aka tortured him, for months that he was going to love his gift and he'd been pretty excited about it, even putting me in a headlock telling me if I didn't stop teasing him about it he'd choke me out. And if that's not true love, I don't know what is.

At the party, the first boy-girl one he'd ever had, he'd invited almost his entire seventh grade class. Because we were in different schools, I didn't know any of the kids, but that was okay as long as I had Jag. When he opened my gift, his face split into a

wide smile and he yelled out, "Sweet, El!" I was thrilled that I'd
made him happy. He came over and punched me in the arm,
putting me once again in a headlock, telling me I was the best
friend ever. When he let me out of his grasp, I couldn't help but
grin back at his excitement.

Who knew that'd be the last time we'd talk for years?

When he opened his next gift, a crappy Hansen CD that
had that ridiculous song on it whose title had way too many
consonants, he then smiled widely at Marie Jackson, those
gorgeous eyes of his beaming in her direction, telling her thank
you, like she'd bought him Nirvana tickets or something. Then he
went to her and shyly kissed her on the cheek. Um, what? I stood
there in shock, watching them looking at each other all googly-
eyed. Again, what?

The rest of the party has become a blur in my mind—I'm
pretty sure my little pre-pubescent self shut it all out, pulling a
Sybil or some shit—and I hardly remember helping Mrs. Jensen
clean up or skating back home afterward. But I do remember
running inside and calling Rebecca, and through my tears telling
her what had happened. She got her dad to drive her over
immediately. She stayed the night and then proceeded to tell me
that there were other fish in the sea, even though we didn't quite
know what that meant, but she'd overheard her older sister telling
it to a friend when a guy had broken up with her, so we figured it
fit the situation and went with it. Rebecca said that Jag Jensen was
a jerk and that he'd be sorry one day for what he'd done to me. We
giggled for the longest time about all the mean things we could do
to Marie Jackson, including sneaking into her room and short-
sheeting her bed or pulling a Fifty-Two Card Pickup *times two* on
her (hey, we were eleven), until Dad stuck his head into my room
and threatened to take Rebecca home if we didn't get quiet. We
drifted off to sleepy snickers and whispered visions of Marie's
having to pick up every card in both decks.

I managed to cry myself to sleep each night thereafter for
the next month. My heart hurt because I knew that something had

changed in Jag's and my relationship. Maybe it was the fact that he was kissing other girls. Duh. Oh, and it also could've been that every time I'd ridden my skateboard over to his house during that time, he was either gone or Marie was over doing homework with him. The few times I had caught him at home, he'd made up some lame excuse that he had something important to do.

I was devastated. Thank God Rebecca had been there for me or I don't know what I'd have done. Probably most definitely pulled a Sybil and developed multiple personalities. That or turned completely girly like Marie, trying to catch Jag's attention. Oh, what fun that would've been.

Chapter 5

I was sixteen when I fell in love with Jag for real.

By that time, I hadn't talked to him for five years.

Five years.

And, God, had it hurt.

Of course, I'd kept tabs on him during that time, but it'd only added to my heartache. I'd discovered that he and Marie Jackson had lasted a good two weeks, which in the seventh grade is the equivalent of an adult year of dating you know, but after their breakup, he was off and running, seemingly "dating" every hot girl in his grade and even a few eighth graders, which took him to celebrity status amongst his peers. As the years passed, I'd heard of the relationships he'd had with several of the most beautiful girls in school including the homecoming queen, the cheer captain, the head of the debate team and the yearbook staff editor.

All of which broke my heart in two.

I'd seen him pitch when I'd gone to baseball games, but never had the nerve to tell him afterward that he'd done a good job. Catching glimpses of him here and there over the years either in the neighborhood or at school was particularly painful. Oh, he'd wave from afar whenever he saw me, which just seemed to make things worse, and I'd wave back if he'd caught me looking, but what usually happened was I acted like I hadn't seen him and just carried on.

The hallways at school were even worse, seeing him with his arm thrown around the shoulders of whichever hottie he was dating at the moment, observing how the girls looked so smug walking beside him as if they were the queen of the world, like they'd staged a coup on the previous girlfriend to win him over, which probably wasn't far from what'd happened.

And, oh, how I'd wished I'd been in their place.

Our verbal drought continued until a day in late March of my sophomore year when I was sitting on a silver-painted rail in the parking lot after track practice waiting for my mom to pick me up since my car was in the shop getting the windows tinted. A rowdy group of sophomore and junior boys was hanging around, all of us just chatting it up, when Jag drove up in his dusk blue '69 Camaro with white racing stripes on the hood, most kickass car ever, and asked if I had a ride. I almost fell off the rail when he'd spoken to me. Then I had one of those *look behind me to make sure he was actually talking to me* moments, then pointed to myself to confirm I was who he'd meant to address. You know what I'm talking about, like the scene from *Sixteen Candles* when Jake pulls up to the church and Samantha doesn't know he's there for her, one of my top ten favorite romantic movie scenes ever by the way. Anyway, yeah, that was me. When I finally got my wits about me, I told him my mom was coming to pick me up, but he told me to call her and let her know he'd take me home.

I looked at him for a couple seconds before making up my mind. Hm. Wait for Mom or get a ride from the hottest senior in school?

My fingers couldn't dial her number fast enough. I waved at the group of guys as I got in Jag's cool-as-hell car, noticing the look of awe on their faces as we drove away.

"So." Jag looked over at me.

My face flushed. What was there to say after five years? I had no idea.

So I rallied.

"So?" I tugged the hem of my track shorts down a little. Damn. Had they always been this ridiculously short? Jeez.

"So how've you been?" he asked, obviously noticing my nervousness as he smirked, glancing down at my hands.

"Um, good."

"Yeah?"

"Yeah." We drove in silence for a few minutes, the guy singing on the radio telling us to hate him today and tomorrow.

Wow. This wasn't awkward to the max at all.

"I, uh, saw you race the other day. Not bad, El." He smiled over at me.

El. He still called me El after five years.

Five years.

Did he still deserve to get to call me that? Of course he did. He'd been with me through a lot. And I was sure he had no idea how much our not talking had devastated me since I'd never let him in on my complete and utter adoration of him. That or our impending nuptials, of course.

"Thanks." I pushed some hair that'd fallen out of my ponytail behind my ear. I was sure I looked fab since I'd just gotten out of practice. Yeesh.

But, God, was he hot. He was now eighteen and had bulked up nicely. He was well over six feet tall, and although he was still kind of lanky, the muscles in his arms were quite nice to look at. His chest had filled out too and I could see the outline of his tight abs through the baseball shirt he wore. I could also see the definition of his thighs through his white uniform pants. Wow. His jaw had squared, which cast a damned movie star aura about him. His eyes were just as astonishing a blue as they'd always been and I saw that that one shock of his dark hair still hung adorably in them.

I'd grown up a lot too—my mom had made sure to feminize me some once my brothers had all left for college by making me wear a little makeup—and even though I was still thin,

I'd actually developed boobs that I never thought I'd get. At 5'8" I was taller than most of my friends and my long, brown hair had developed auburn highlights from my being out on the track in the sun after school each day. My tanned skin made my green eyes stand out more, but a consequence of spending so much time in the sun was the stupid freckles that dotted my nose. Running hurdles had made my legs stronger, so I guessed I looked okay, or at least some of the boys yelling, "Nice legs!" at me when I wore shorts or skirts to school and the whispers I heard in the hallways about my being hot—this made me crack the hell up they'd say that about me—made me think I was at least passable.

Sitting there in his car with Jag was so surreal, that when he asked if it was okay if we stopped at a fast food place where a lot of the kids hung out, I just stared at him.

"El?"

I snapped out of my haze and asked, "Huh?" because I was smooth that way.

He smiled back at me before turning to watch the road again. "Care if we stop to get a float before going home?"

"Float?" I couldn't grasp what he was saying, like being in his presence stripped me of all cognitive ability. And I couldn't stop staring! Gah!

"Yeah. You know, root beer float?" He grinned over at me as he shifted gears on the car probably thinking I was mental.

"Oh, yeah. That'd be fuper." Oh, dear God.

"Fuper?" He muffled a snicker, looking over at me confused.

"Yeah, I, uh, meant to say 'fun' but then 'super' snuck its way in there too."

Yep. I was officially an idiot. I turned my head to look out my window, bringing my left hand to shield my face so he couldn't see me as I rolled my eyes and shook my head at my stupid self. Ugh. Kill me now.

"Fuper it is," he said with a chuckle, reaching over to pull my hand away from my face. I looked over at him to see him wink at me before smirking again which only made me want to put my hand up to cover my face again.

Despite my dumbass tendencies, I was thrilled to be hanging out with him again, and not because he was hot, though that didn't hurt matters any, but because he was Jag. *My* Jag. And he was back. At least for now.

We stopped at a little fast food joint and went inside, sitting in a booth. There were a bunch of other kids there from school, and I thought that for him to actually take me there and not be embarrassed to be seen with a sophomore was pretty cool. When the waitress came by, he ordered our customary root beer floats.

A few of the guys in the place came up to talk to him, smiling and saying hi to me. Some even knew my name. Huh. When the waitress brought our drinks, they left, telling Jag they'd see him at practice the next day.

"So what have you been up to?"

Hm. What had I been up to? I wondered if I could, in one concise paragraph, tell him all that'd happened in the past five years.

"In the past five years or lately?" I asked, spooning some ice cream into my mouth.

He chuckled. "Let's start with lately and work our way back."

I twisted my lips to the side, thinking of all that'd been going on lately. "Rebecca and I barely made it out alive in Chem I the other day because Zach Darren thought it'd be fun to point a test tube at us that had potassium chlorate in it after he'd dropped in a gummy bear."

He raised an eyebrow as he looked over at me. "Don't those pretty much shoot out fire?"

"Yeah. So I didn't feel bad at all when I grabbed the fire extinguisher off the wall and sprayed that foam stuff all over him."

He laughed, shaking his head.

"Oh, and Rebecca and I also got tickets to see Three Days Grace…"

Looking impressed, he commented, "Yeah? How'd you manage that?"

"We heard that Bobby Winfield had a couple tickets but he was selling them for, like, three hundred dollars each. We didn't have that much money, so we made a drug deal with him."

He choked on his drink then narrowed his eyes at me suspiciously.

"Calm down. We told him we could score him some coke for the tickets because Rebecca's dad's a cop and she could steal some from the evidence room. So we mixed baking soda with some of Rebecca's little brother's crushed up Ritalin pills and traded him."

The corner of Jag's mouth twitched as he shook his head again. "You two are bad."

"Hey, the next weekend after the concert, he told us it was the 'best shit,'" I did air quotes here, "he'd ever had."

He took a bite of his ice cream, his eyes crinkling at the corners as he looked at me. "Anything else?"

"Well," I drew that word out into at least three syllables wondering if I really should tell him more of the stuff we'd been up to. Man, people were just dumb to ever mess with us, I realized with a snicker. Taking a deep breath, I informed him of Rebecca's and my chicanery. "When Sissy Jacobs stole Rebecca's boyfriend, Andy, at the first of the year, we filled her locker with tampons, so when Andy walked with her after class, and she opened it, they all spilled out which embarrassed the hell out of her. Um, we taped an air horn to the bottom of Coach Miller's chair on a test day, so when he sat down, it went off. He fell out of his chair and was laughing so hard, he called off the test." I twisted my mouth again and rolled my eyes to the ceiling thinking of other things we'd done. "Oh! When Brian Jones called me a bitch last semester because I wouldn't go out with him, we had some friends keep him busy before history class—which Coach Hendricks teaches and he doesn't give a crap about anything but football, so we knew we'd get away with it—anyway, we put plastic wrap across the door with superglue all over it about forehead level, and Brian walked right into it."

Jag snorted. "Wondered why he shaved his head."

I laughed. "He called me a lot worse names than bitch after that. But it was worth it."

"Damn, El. You two are devious," he said. "That it?"

I thought for a few seconds. "Uh, the secretary wouldn't let Rebecca call home when she felt sick a couple weeks ago, so we wrapped her phone in duct tape after school. And when Candice Yates got her new car a month ago, she gave everyone a ride to the track but Rebecca and me, so we Saran Wrapped it to a light pole in the parking lot so she couldn't get into it the next day."

Wow. Guess Rebecca and I'd really made some headway since our days of scheming to short-sheet beds or play Fifty-Two Card Pickup.

"Remind me never to get on your bad side," he said smiling crookedly at me, which nearly stopped my breath.

I stared at him a couple seconds before realizing he'd spoken.

Oh. Yeah. Conversation, El. Have one. You know, that thing where you open your mouth and use your vocal cords to create sounds, which are actually things called words. People use these to communicate. It's cool. Try it.

"I hadn't thought about it before, but I guess we really are pretty ruthless." I looked at him in surprise at my confession, which made him smile even more crookedly.

Be. Still. My. Heart.

"Who were all those guys hanging around you in the parking lot today?" he then asked between spoonfuls of his float.

I shrugged. "Just mostly guys who got out of practice, I guess. I mean, some of them are in track, but I think some of them are golfers too," I said, then took a drink.

He was looking at me when I put my glass down, his eyes turning a dark navy. I frowned wondering what was wrong. He reached his hand out toward my face and I slowly backed my head away as his hand slowly kept inching forward. I would've laughed at any other time, but since I hadn't talked to him in ages and had no clue what he was doing, I was wary. I finally stopped moving back still frowning at him, curiously wondering what the hell was going on. When I finally sat still long enough, his fingers cupped my chin and he stroked his thumb across the top of my lip then he pulled his hand away, stuck the pad of his thumb into his mouth and sucked on it. My eyes got huge at this wildly erotic gesture. I realized I must've had foam above my lip and he'd wiped it away then licked it. Whoa.

I stared at him for a second, the heated look in his eyes throwing me way off balance since I was new at this seduction stuff or whatever it was. Good grief, I had no idea what was happening to my body right then, but I remember thinking he could do that any time he wanted if it made me feel that way. Holy smokes.

I must've looked like the big idiot virgin I was right then too, all uptight and astonished, but not because Jag made me feel that way. He just gave me his sexy half smirk then carried on, spooning a big chunk of ice cream into his mouth, his dark eyes still on mine, while I sat there all heated and flustered and panting.

Try getting back into normal conversation after an incident like that.

But we did, well, I finally did after my pulse rate dropped from eight billion beats per second, and it was nice to be starting our friendship back up again. It'd felt as if I'd had a hole inside for all those years and I now found that Jag was just the thing to patch it up.

When he dropped me off at home, for a reason I didn't question, he volunteered to pick me up every day for school and take me home after his baseball practice and my track practice. I know I could've driven my own car, but I was no fool. Spending time with Jag was the best thing I had going and I didn't want to blow it.

A couple weeks after our friendship had started up again, he came by on a Saturday night. "El, come with me. I wanna show you something."

I ran out of the house so fast to go with him that I barely heard Mom remind me that I needed to put away my laundry. Nice, huh? Hey, she always put my brothers' laundry away, so I think I deserved one bye on the chore just that once.

On the way, we stopped to get root beer floats to go then Jag drove to a kind of lookout point.

"This is where I come when I need to think."

"It's beautiful up here," I said in approval, feeling honored that he'd share this place with me since he said he'd never told anyone else about it.

We sat on the hood of his car leaning back against the windshield, looking out at the abundance of sparkling city lights, which was an awesome sight.

"What do you wanna do after graduating?" he asked, staring out at the twinkling skyline.

"Well, being the trainer for the football team has been fun, aside from all the stinky, sweaty guys, but it's seriously made me consider going into sports medicine," I informed him.

He chuckled. "That's cool. I think you'd be great in that field."

I smiled. "Thanks. What about you?" I asked looking over at him, still in awe that we were sitting there together after having been apart for so long.

He sighed. "When I was little I wanted to play in a band like my dad did."

I knew this already because he'd said so when we were young and, man, he could play a guitar crazy good. So could his sister. He'd tried teaching me when we were younger but my fingers weren't long enough to hit some of the chords, so I opted to just listening to him play.

"Then I thought about being a professional skateboarder." I smacked his arm knowing he was being a dork. "Hey! When I got my kickflip down, I thought I was gonna be the next Tony Hawk!"

"Whatever." I chuckled.

"Then being a gigolo crossed my mind."

I almost did a spit take with my float as my hand came up to cover my mouth. I looked at him and rolled my eyes exaggeratedly. "Well, I'm sure you'd never go broke."

He quirked an eyebrow at me as he grinned. "You think? Man, El, if I didn't know any better, I'd think you were saying I'm hot."

Of course, he was hot! And, of course, my face turned every shade of red imaginable, which made him grin even more.

He leaned into me, knocking my shoulder playfully with his. "No, but it's been insane with all these coaches looking at me from all these colleges. There've even been some pro scouts that have come out."

I knew he was good, but hadn't realized he was that good. Dang.

"So go pro," I said with a shrug.

He laughed. "You make it sound so easy."

"You're good, Jag. That's why it'd *be* easy." He dragged a hand over his face looking a little worried. "What is it?" I asked.

"It's just that it's a lot of pressure. If I go pro right out of high school, I have a better chance of going to the majors. But my parents want me to get a degree." He frowned. "After three years, I can go pro, but the odds of being drafted go way down." He looked scared and uncertain just then, something I'd never seen him be. Jag was always confident, it seemed.

I boldly took his hand in mine, lacing our fingers together, trying to reassure him as he'd done for me once. "You're good, Jag. I'll bet you could go pro any time you wanted." I knocked my shoulder back into his. "It's your destiny to be awesome. C'mon, with a name like Jagger Knox Jensen, you're going places."

He snorted at that, still looking a little doubtful.

I tried taking his mind off of his worries. "Look at it this way. One day when I'm a physical therapist or whatever, I'll get to take care of your rickety, old body when your arm wears out from striking out everyone."

"You wanna take care of my body, huh?" he asked, squeezing my hand, looking over at me with a wicked gleam in his eyes, which totally left me flabbergasted.

"I, uh, well, I… yeah," I stammered then grimaced, not knowing what else to say. I bowed my head, embarrassed as could be, stirring the straw around in what was left of my float. When I looked up at him, a gasp left me at the sexier-than-hell look he sported, his half grin in full effect while he watched me, and all I could do was sit there and be stupefied. Heavy on the stup. At that crooked grin on his face, a shiver ran through me, which I'm sure he noticed, since his damned grin got even bigger.

"So fucking cute," he mumbled while shaking his head then he gave me a genuine smile and winked at me.

Now, I'd read a lot of romance books, some I was sure that if Mom knew about they would've sent her on a cleaning frenzy for days trying to keep her mind off what her only daughter had been mentally digesting, but I never knew that what was written in those books was freaking real. At Jag's wink, my insides did a flip-flop, my heart was pounding in my chest and I was so heated that I was tempted to pour the remainder of my float over my head to cool off.

All this from a wink and a smile. Wow.

After that night, I finally got my bearings and decided to stop being an amateur. Jag was getting a kick out of keeping me off balance with his flirtatiousness. Well, two could play that game, right? It wasn't like I'd never flirted before.

A few days later, we sat in a booth at our little burger place, drinking root beer floats again. And here went nothing. While we were talking, I raised an eyebrow at him then picked up my glass to take a drink, planning to get some foam on my lip again then provocatively swipe my tongue over it to put Mr. Hot Stuff in his place. Good intentions and all that, right? So just as I tipped the glass, a huge glob of ice cream slammed into my lips causing me to gasp as the drink went into my mouth.

So… if choking's considered sexy, I nailed that bitch.

But, sadly, it's not, so there I sat, coughing my lungs up, sounding like a damned seal on steroids. The next thing I knew, Jag had gotten up coming to sit next to me then proceeded to pound me on the back with the force of a jackhammer asking if I was okay. Ugh. So much for my being the next Bond girl with all the sex appeal I exuded. I finally got over my fit, Jag went back to his seat, and we finished our floats amidst friendly chatter. Thank God he hadn't realized what I'd been trying to do. That seduction shit was hard!

Now, while hanging out with Jag was all well and good, I couldn't help wondering why he wanted to spend time with me. God knew I'd crushed on him forever, so could it have been that my feelings were being reciprocated? I mean, who spends that much time with someone if there's not an eensy-weensy bit of interest, right? He'd remained flirty but hadn't tried anything with me, so I wasn't sure what the deal was. Maybe he just missed the comfort of our friendship. I decided not to question it and just go with the flow. If it ain't broke, don't fix it, yeah?

"Watch the ball, El!" Jag was pitching to me and I was batting. Oh, boy. We were at the high school field a couple weeks later on a Saturday when no one was there, just messing around and he was trying to show me some of the ins and outs of America's favorite pastime. "Keep your eye on it then swing!" He did his wind up and sent a pitch my way.

"Ahhh! Why can't I hit it?" I shrieked, after I'd swung and missed. Again. For like the twentieth time. I stomped my foot like a spoiled brat. He was taking it way easy on me by throwing me tosses that a ten-year-old boy could hit, yet I couldn't. Damn it.

"Gotta keep your eye on the ball, babe." He chuckled.

"You've said that a million times! I'm keeping my eye on the ball and I keep missing! This sucks!" I was pissed now. I was a decent athlete and not being able to hit the damned ball was a blow to my ego. "Okay, hotshot, come with me," I said, leaning the bat against the backstop then walking toward the track.

Jag came jogging up behind me. "Gonna teach me to hurdle, huh?" He snorted.

"Yep. It's not as easy as it looks." I gave him a dirty look out of the side of my eye.

When we got to the track, I made him stretch with me so we wouldn't pull any muscles then I said, "Jog a lap with me."

"Sure thing, Coach," he said with another chuckle which got him another dirty look.

He kept up easily with me and when we got back to where we'd started, I took him into the hurdle lanes. "Okay, let's race."

"El, do you really think this is fair?"

Well, that was nice of him. He thought that since I ran the hurdles I'd probably beat him. "Oh, I think you'll be able to keep up with me a little." I was in a standing hamstring stretch, my legs crossed at the ankles as I bent at my waist, hanging my hands down to touch my toes. His burst of laughter made me look up at him from the side. "What?"

"You think *I'll* have a hard time keeping up with *you*?" he asked with a sneer.

I slowly stood back up to glare at him. Was he serious? "Oh, it's on, Jensen."

"Show me the way, Love," he said with a snicker.

I put him in a lane at the starting line then took my lane two places over. "Okay, when I say 'Go!' take off," I said. "If you think you can keep up." I gave him a smirk of my own. I'd just won the last two track meets in the 100-meter hurdles, so I was pretty sure I had this in the bag, because even if he was faster, I'd still win with technique. "Ready?" He nodded back with that smug grin. Jerk. I got in my stance as if I had a starting block. "On your mark… get set… go!" I shouted and took off.

Now, when I raced, I was focused and in the zone. All I saw was ten hurdles in front of me until I got to the finish line. But this time, I was hyperaware of Jag, and as I reached the seventh hurdle, I sensed that I was alone. As in seriously alone. No other sound but my own breathing alone. I stopped before the eighth hurdle and turned around to see him sprawled out on the track between the fourth and fifth hurdles.

"Jag!" I ran back to check if he was okay. When I got to him, he was face down on the track and cussing up a storm. "You okay?" I asked, biting on my lips so I wouldn't laugh at him.

"Fuck!" he yelled as he turned over.

Oh, this was too funny. "Do I, uh, need to call nine-waah-waah? Do you need a waahmbulance?" I snorted, looking down at him.

He glared at me from where he lay then knifed up quickly and grabbed my hand pulling me down on top of him.

"Hey!" I shrieked with a laugh.

And it was at that time that he grabbed my face firmly in his hands, pulling my face to his and soundly pressed his lips to mine.

Remember the *Beauty and the Beast* sparkles and fireworks? Yep. Totally happened. It was amazing.

He pulled back from me with a heated look, his eyes going all dark navy on me, then he smiled, probably at the stunned look on my face, before turning us over to where he was on top of me then he came back in to dazzle me again. His lips were so soft yet demanding on mine and the kiss was so heated and making me so damned hot that I knew I was probably melting the rubber track beneath me. Dear God it felt wonderful. My hands went up to knot in his dark hair as I pulled him closer, not able to get enough of him.

I'd never been kissed before, well, unless you counted our first kiss when I was five and he was seven, but did that stop me? Hell no. I wanted, no, *needed* this contact with him, and boy, did I go for broke. This time his tongue edged out and softly touched my bottom lip, and when I opened my mouth in a gasp, he slid it inside, finding my own, to tangle lightly with it. Wow.

Best. First. Kiss. Ever.

When we finally came up for air, my head was spinning, both of us breathing heavily, and I couldn't help the sappy grin I wore.

"Wow," I whispered.

"Yeah, wow," he answered back, pulling away and looking down at me confused.

"Best first kiss ever," I mumbled breathlessly, looking up into his eyes in a haze.

The confusion left his face as if he'd been waiting to hear that he was my first and a proud grin replaced it. Guys. Jeez.

After that day, I only brought up the fact that I'd beaten him in hurdles a time or two… or ten. But that memory was *way* overshadowed by the fact that it was also the day of my first kiss. Of *our* first kiss. And I'd never forget it as long as I lived.

"Hey, beautiful," Jag said when he drove up in the parking lot a couple days later. "You ready?"

My face instantly flushed at his endearment and especially so when the boys hanging around whistled and made sounds of approval at it. Ugh. An inner construction worker must be hidden inside all males.

"Hey, handsome," I replied shyly after getting in the car. God. My face got so hot you could've fried a damned egg on it at what I thought was pretty brazen behavior on my part.

Jag looked over and grinned at me, his straight white teeth in his tanned face making him look like an Abercrombie & Fitch model. Lord, the guy was just hotter than freaking hot.

While driving we talked about the usual things, how practice had gone and how school was that day before an unusual silence hit. After we'd hit a stoplight, Jag finally broke it when we got the green.

"Gotta question, uh, for you," he said as he shifted gears. Was he nervous? Hm.

"Question? Yes, Jag, Bigfoot *is* real." I snorted at the look on his face.

"Ellen." He raised an eyebrow, looking over and giving me a gimlet eye.

"Jagger," I said, mocking his look.

"I need to ask you a serious question, El," he replied with a sigh, looking back at the road.

Oh, crap. The sober look on his face worried me. And when I glanced out the window behind him, I saw that we were heading home and not to one of the hangouts. This *must* be serious. Yikes.

"Um, okay. Go ahead." Dang it. I could feel the sweat forming on my brow. God, was he going to ask if it was okay if I started driving myself to school again? Was he tired of me? I felt my stomach clench up. I knew it'd been too good to be true. Seriously, why the hell would a senior want to spend time with a sophomore anyway? An inexperienced sophomore at that. I'd always known the other shoe would drop on this thing we had going on. And damn it if tears didn't start welling in my eyes.

We pulled into my driveway and he turned off the engine. I sat facing forward like a statue, focusing on trying to breathe normally. Oh, and blinking my eyes rapidly a couple times to make sure the tears didn't fall. Shit! He probably thought I was having some kind of fricking seizure now. Guess that was better than his knowing he was about to break my heart. Again.

For a few seconds he messed with his key ring that I'd given him a few weeks before that hung from the ignition switch. It held a picture that my mom had taken of us when Jag and I were little. In the photo, I was crying because I'd dropped my ice cream cone and Jag was holding his out for me to have. How friggin' sweet was that? He stared at the picture for a few more seconds then looked over at me, throwing his right arm over the back of my seat. I guess it was then that he saw me struggling to keep from crying.

"Hey," he said, his left hand moving to my chin, turning my face toward his.

I didn't want to look at him. If he was going to tell me this was over, whatever *this* was, I'd rather not have to look in those beautiful blue eyes of his, so I closed my own as a stupid tear rolled down my face.

And here's what was going through my head as we sat there: just give it to me fast, Jag. Bam! Drop that hammer and let me get out of the car so I can go cry in the safety of my own room. Do it! Quick! Stop drawing things out, damn it!

But when he didn't say anything, my curiosity got the better of me and I peeked at him with one eye. *One eye!* Dear God. I'm sure I looked like an idiot with my face all scrunched up trying to see what was going on.

His mouth twitched as one side of it drew up in a half smirk. Really? What was so funny about this?

"What's so funny about this?" I snapped opening both of my eyes as the anger finally hit me and I pushed his hand off my chin. Just end it already!

"Well, you kinda looked like Popeye there for a sec." He barked out a laugh.

Yeah, this was just hilarious. He was going to tell me that we'd no longer be spending time together and he was getting a big heehaw out of it. Nice.

"Did not!" I huffed out, pissed. Well, good thing was, at least I no longer had the urge to cry.

"Yeah, you did." He snorted as he reached out and wiped my stray tear away with his thumb. "Hey, what's this all about?" He then frowned getting serious again.

I huffed out a sigh and closed my eyes again seeking some courage. Then a fantastic idea hit me. *I'd* be the one to break things off so that my amount of hurt would be less than if he did it. And that idea? Freaking brilliant!

I sniffed before taking a deep breath then stared straight ahead. "Well, you know, Jag, this has been fun, hanging out and all."

I heard him shift in his seat, so I chanced a look at him out of the side of my eye. Oh, boy. I had his full attention now. His arm was still over the back of my seat but I could feel, yes *feel,* the tension that immediately hung in the air and also that he'd now moved a smidgen away from me. I looked down at my hands in my lap, my fingers tangling nervously. And then stupid me ventured forward. "But I'm really getting behind on some things, so I thought it'd probably be for the best that I start driving myself to school now."

He was quiet for so long, I didn't know what to do. Twiddling my thumbs came to mind but I nixed that dumb idea right away. When I finally looked at him, he was looking at me through narrowed eyes as if trying to figure me out.

"Did you now?" he said, his question sounding dangerous. Yikes.

Did I now? Did I now, what?

"Um, did I now, what?" I asked like a nitwit.

"You thought it'd be for the best…" And the look on his face. Dang. Did he want to strangle me? Kiss me? Both of those ideas were too unnerving to even think about right then.

I decided to stay the course I'd been on, stay strong, still trying to cover myself, not willing to be left brokenhearted by him again. No, I'd just break my own damned heart instead. "Yes, you're probably getting tired of me anyway, right?"I asked feebly. So much for staying strong.

I looked at him again and those eyes of his were cutting through me like a knife. I swore sparks were flying from them.

"You think I'm tired of you?"

I pushed that one piece of hair that always escaped my ponytail behind my ear nervously, looking back at the windshield as I chewed on my bottom lip. God, this was so intense. I wasn't sure what to do, what to think. All I wanted was for him to get this over with so I could go inside my house, grab a pint of Chocolate Therapy and a spoon, and go to my room to cry my eyes out into my ice cream over losing him again.

"Aren't you?" I whispered.

I mean, come on. Here was Jag Jensen, baseball player extraordinaire, the guy every girl in school was in love with, sitting here with me, plain old Ellen Love, bookworm to boot and somewhat decent trackster. What could he want with *me*?

He burst out laughing again and I looked at him in shock. *Now* what was so funny?

"How could I ever be tired of you, El? You and these cute-as-hell freckles?" He then dotted several of them on my nose with his finger to my horror.

I swiped away his hand. "Stop that!" I said with a scowl, but he kept right on poking at my nose. Ugh! "Jag, if you know what's good for you, you'll keep your finger away from my fucking nose!"

This only made him laugh more and, of course, keep on jabbing at them. I put my hands up, trying to block his, but then I couldn't help but laugh along with him. The jerk.

"Quit! I'm gonna punch your lights out if you don't stop!" I yelled through my giggles.

Then he grabbed my face and kissed me. Hard. And I loved it. God, I'd never get tired of kissing him. My hands went up to either side of his face, keeping him as close to me as possible as our kiss burned hotter than hot.

"So," he said breathlessly as he pulled away and smoothed that ridiculous piece of hair behind my ear again.

"So," I replied dreamily but just as out of breath, putting my head back against the seat and closing my eyes.

I heard him chuckle. Then he paused before stating, "The, uh, question I was going to ask you…"

I sat up stiffly and turned toward him. Damn! I'd forgotten about the stupid question. My heart started pounding in my chest again as I remembered that he was probably going to tell me he wouldn't be picking me up anymore, didn't want to spend time with me anymore.

He'd moved back fully into his seat and was looking out his side window so he didn't see the panic in my eyes. He turned back toward the front then started fiddling with the gearshift, probably trying to think of a way to let me down easy, not wanting to feel too bad that he was going to kick me to the curb after kissing me like that. Great.

"Well, what I wanted to know was…" He paused as he became really interested in something on the gear knob.

Good God! Spit it out already! End my misery now!

"Would you go to Prom with me?"

Chapter 6

I was almost seventeen when I really, *really* fell in love with Jag.

After that first kiss on the track, well, it seemed that I couldn't keep my lips off of his. I don't think he minded too much, though. And after the question-in-his-car-in-my-driveway-when-I-thought-he-didn't-want-to-see-me-anymore debacle, we were inseparable from that day forward, getting in every moment together before he left for college.

"I think I've narrowed it down to where I want to go," Jag informed my parents and me over dinner one night. The college coaches had been courting him like mad, from one side of the nation to the other. He'd gone on his visits and gotten so many offers, I was surprised that he'd ever be able to make a decision.

"Oh, yeah? Which?" my dad asked.

"Either Oregon State or South Carolina."

Now, having three older brothers who were really into sports, I'd learned a thing or two over the years, so when I heard his choices, I let out a huge snort, making everyone look at me.

"What?" Jag asked narrowing his eyes at me.

"Seriously? It's come down to whether you want to be a Beaver or a 'Cock?" I died laughing especially at the look on my mom's face.

"Ellen Reese Love!" she scolded.

My dad was having a tough time holding in his laughter and he finally gave up the ghost, letting out a snort before Mom gave him a dirty look.

Jag gave me a wicked *you'll pay for this later* look after he'd barked out a laugh at my pronouncement. "Hadn't thought of that, El. Leave it to you…"

And if the make out session Jag and I had before he went home was his way of paying me back for my mascot remark, well he could bring it on any old day.

A week later I sat in history class bored to tears, wishing Coach Hendricks would stop droning on and on about the Civil War when Rebecca made a snorting sound through her nose. I glanced over at her to see that she was looking at the classroom door. I followed her gaze and saw Jag and her boyfriend Ross Thompson (he played catcher for the baseball team, was a senior also, and a good friend of Jag's) making faces at us through the window in the door. I snickered as they put on a little show for us, Ross mimicking Coach Hendricks' teaching and Jag acting like he was falling asleep, which made Rebecca and I giggle, but stop quickly when we realized Coach Hendricks was looking at us. When the guys started acting like they were going down the stairs as they walked in a circle, going lower each time they went round, it was all I could do to keep from bursting out laughing. But the funniest part of all was as they were making their third circle, Mr. Vining, our principal, walked up and stood watching them and their antics, unbeknownst to them. It was a classic moment as they made one more turn and they both finally saw him, arms across his chest, watching how ridiculous they were being, and both their mouths dropped open. Rebecca and I almost fell out of our desks laughing as Mr. Vining pointed down the hallway toward his office and Jag and Ross looked back at us with *Oh shit!* faces.

"Girls? Jensen and Thompson give you a good show?" Coach Hendricks asked gaining our attention.

It was Rebecca's and my turn to sport *Oh shit!* faces then. But Coach Hendricks just chuckled and shook his head before continuing his lecture. Thank God Coach H was cool as hell.

After track practice that day (Rebecca came to watch), she and I jogged over to the baseball field to see our guys. Jag was pitching and I couldn't take my eyes off him. He looked freaking hot wearing his red cap, a white baseball shirt with red sleeves, and white pants with little red stripes. Yum. What can I say? I was a sucker for striped baseball pants especially on him. He threw a pitch and the batter swung, drawing only air.

"Go Jag!" I yelled, sticking my fingers in my mouth and letting out a shrill whistle from where Rebecca and I stood behind the backstop.

Coach Martin cut his eyes at me and I grinned and waved enthusiastically at him. I'd been his aide my freshman year and knew he was all bark and no bite. Well, when it came to me. I knew he was tough on his players because I'd witnessed a couple of his yelling fits, but they all respected him and knew he was a good coach because our team was really dang good.

I looked out at Jag, who'd just caught the ball from Ross who was catching, and saw him grin and shake his head as he looked down at the ground as he walked back to the pitcher's mound. He then got in position, watching Ross's signals, shaking his head the first couple times then he nodded and started his windup. I think he threw a curveball because that sucker seriously had been going straight before it made a huge drop down right as it got to the batter, who swung and missed again.

"That's my boyfriend!" I yelled.

"And that's *my* boyfriend!" Rebecca yelled, pointing at Ross.

Coach Martin shot both of us a sour look and we knew we were treading on thin ice, so giggling like idiots, we climbed the bleachers to watch the rest of practice in silence.

"God, look at Ross's ass, El. Isn't it the cutest thing ever?"

I laughed. "Well, I'm kinda partial to Jag's, you know."

"He's got a cute ass too," she said with a snicker.

I leaned back on the bleachers soaking in the sun's rays. "So, Prom. Have you decided?" I asked, holding a hand over my eyes to shade them as I looked at her.

"Yeah. I'm gonna," she answered.

I sat up quickly, a little surprised. "You are?"

"Yep." She smiled at me. "I love him, El."

"Wow."

"Yeah."

I sat pensively for a few minutes, letting that settle in a bit. When I'd come to terms with it, I said, "I love Jag too. I know I've always loved him. I think I'm ready too."

She nodded in agreement. She and I had talked about having sex since we'd first figured out what it was, so this was nothing new, and we'd both agreed that if we were really in love, that it'd be okay if it felt right. But now we were seriously talking about losing our virginity on Prom night, which was serious business.

"We'll have to prepare, you know," she added.

"Yeah. We'll have to make an appointment, right? I'm kinda scared, Bec." I thought I was ready, but I wasn't really sure. That was some heavy stuff to deal with!

"We'll go together, El. It'll be fine," she said, taking my hand and squeezing it before letting it go.

"El!" Jag yelled at me from the field. Practice was over and I hadn't even noticed.

I looked down to see him standing on the other side of the backstop, beckoning me by curling a finger several times.

I jumped up and ran down the bleachers to him. In a totally nostalgic move, he put his face to the fence and stuck his lips through the chain link, puckering up when I made it to him. I laughed before smashing my lips to his.

"Fireworks?" he asked, pulling away then looking up and around before looking down at me and winking.

"Totally," I said with a chuckle.

God, I really truly loved him. And that was all I needed to know that I was ready to give myself wholly to him.

So Jag and I did the whole prom thing, and it had been so much fun. He'd picked me up looking all dapper in his black tux with the vest and cumberbund that matched my dress in color. He looked so good that my knees almost buckled when I came downstairs and saw him standing in the living room waiting for me. Wow. He was so handsome. That boy could clean up nicely! The grin on his face told me that he'd appreciated how I'd looked too. Well, that and his actually telling me how beautiful I looked.

And, God, I *so* loved my dress! It was a frou-frou, sea-foam green monstrosity and it was *fabulous*. It looked like something Scarlett O'Hara would've worn, ball gown skirt, sweetheart neckline, strapless and I loved it so much, I couldn't even be bothered to be upset over the way it went wacko on me when I got in Jag's car, the bell skirt and crinoline petticoat practically flipping up to where I could hardly see out of the windshield. Thank God I wasn't the one driving.

But before we'd left to attend the fun-filled fete, our parents had had to take a bazillion pictures of us. Jag's parents had ridden with him to my house and planned to walk home after having dinner with my parents. And, man, I had no idea there were that many poses out there. If I didn't end up having to take ibuprofen for my aching muscles from some of the positions they'd put me in, I'd need it anyway because my cheeks were sore from smiling so damned much.

At Prom we'd danced our ever-loving hearts out the entire time only stopping a few times to get some punch. Make that heavily-saturated-with-whatever-liquor-Derek Bradshaw-had-sneaked-out-of-his-house punch, but I think the adrenaline from dancing kept us from getting overly buzzed. I'd been drunk exactly once before when Rebecca and I'd decided to make "Long Island iced teas" our freshman year when her parents had been out of town and I'd spent the night with her. I quote the drink name because pouring fifteen different types of liquor into a glass of Coke does not an LIit make. But I learned an invaluable lesson that night: after one glass, who gives a shit anymore. Your taste buds sure don't. Lesson two, you ask? Don't mix fifteen different types of liquor in a glass of Coke until your taste buds don't give a shit anymore. Ick.

Jag had gotten us a room at the hotel where Prom was being held. I couldn't believe that Mom and Dad had actually agreed to let me stay, but when I'd told them that Rebecca and Ross had a room there too, it'd kind of sealed the deal. Well, that and they loved Jag, so it was pretty much a homerun.

Rebecca and I were both nervous for the after-Prom gig, as should be expected. In preparation, we'd gone the month before to Planned Parenthood and gotten on birth control. I felt bad about not telling Mom, but I just couldn't fathom talking with her about it, knowing it'd probably make her cry and I just didn't want to deal with that… ever. Rebecca and I had also read up on everything we could find about "doing it," as we so expertly called it, from how much it would hurt to reading the article, "How to Keep Him Completely Satisfied in Bed: 50 Kinky Sex Moves

Every Girl Should Know" from one of those chick magazines. She and I walked away from that one scratching our heads.

Regardless of my preparation, I was still a bundle of scared little girl by the time Jag and I made it to our room around midnight.

Once there, I excitedly explored everything, from running (yes, running in my humongo dress) out to the balcony to squealing over the TV in the bathroom. Jag had followed me the first couple of times through (I'd held his hand and yanked on it pulling him along with me) but he'd finally sat down on the bed tired of seeing all the cool stuff, I guessed. After my fourth time through, he called my name, and I came out of the bathroom where I'd been playing with the TV to see him sitting on the edge of the bed. He used his pointer finger, hooking it at me a few times, summoning me to him. I walked to him, and he moved his legs apart so I could stand between them. He placed his hands on my hips and pressed the top of his head against my stomach for several seconds before looking up at me. "What's up with you, El? All of a sudden you act like you're scared to death of me."

Oh. He'd figured out that I'd been stalling.

"I'm not scared of you," I whispered. My heart was about to pound out of my chest. I really wasn't scared of *him*; I was just terrified of what I'd planned for the night.

He arched an eyebrow and raised his hand to push that cute hunk of hair out of his eyes, his hand going back to rest on my waist. "Then why are you avoiding me?" He looked up at me with those brilliant blue eyes of his so full of concern.

I reached down and messed with his bowtie. God, he looked so good in his tux. "I'm not."

That made him raise both eyebrows. "Liar."

His saying that made *my* eyebrows raise up in surprise.

He cupped my face and pulled me down to him, forcing me to put my hands on his thighs for balance, and put his forehead against mine. "I got the room because I knew it'd be late. I also knew some idiot would probably spike the punch, so it might not be safe for me to drive." He touched his lips to mine then pulled back and said, "I also told your dad this. That's probably why your parents said it was okay for you to stay with me."

I stood up slowly and I think my mouth froze into a permanent O as I stared at him, embarrassed that he'd asked my dad if I could stay. Duh. I *knew* it'd been too easy when I'd asked my parents.

"What? Did you think I got this room because I expected you to 'put out'?" He snorted as I still stood just staring down at him. "Although I did love this just now… you bending down… your tits right in my face." He reached for me with a smirk.

That shook me out of my daze and I frowned pulling away from him. It stung a little that he hadn't planned to sleep with me. I mean, I'd decided to give him something that I held very precious and he hadn't even given it a second thought.

His eyes got soft and he grabbed my wrist and pulled me onto his lap. I was pissed until I couldn't help but giggle as he fought to keep the skirt of my dress from flipping up everywhere. When he finally got it under control, he looked at me and shook his head, his lips twitching at the corners. "You really thought that's what I wanted, didn't you? El, I'd never put pressure on you for that; you know that, right?"

I bit the inside of my cheek and frowned again, knowing he was right. Of course, he'd never pressure me. Boy, I felt like a dumbass. "I feel like a dumbass."

He snorted again. "Why?"

"That's kinda what I thought. Not that you'd pressure me, but that it'd be what you expected. But I'm actually the one who made plans for us to, you know, sleep together." I looked sheepishly at him. "Now I feel like *I'm* the one who's put pressure on *you*." I gnawed on my bottom lip feeling bad for putting him through this.

He barked out a laugh. "Oh, it's no pressure on me at all, believe me." He tucked a stray lock of hair behind my ear and looked at me, his eyes beaming. "Listen, El. I love you. I do."

I stared at him for a beat. "Di— did you just say that you love me?" I whispered. He nodded slowly, watching me.

He loved me?

Oh my God! He loved me!

My eyes teared up. "I love you too, Jag," I confessed. "I think I always have."

He chuckled pulling me into him, wrapping his arms tightly around me and tucking my head under his chin. He kissed the top of my head and rested his chin there again before he spoke. "That's good because I feel the same. And I hope you understand what I'm gonna tell you. God, this will go against every fucking Mancode there is." He moved back and rubbed a hand over his face then looked at me out of the side of his eyes, a little chagrined. "Hell, they'd probably revoke my Man Card if they heard what I'm going to tell you," he mumbled. He sighed deeply before facing me full on. "But I wouldn't try anything with you right now, El. You're only sixteen. That's so damned young."

I sat up straight and pulled back from him at that. "It's not that young. And I'll be seventeen in two weeks," I said indignantly, the humiliation of the situation making my stomach clench. Then a thought hit me that made my heart sink. "I'll bet you had sex by the time you were sixteen," I said quietly.

He sighed again. "It's different for guys." When my body went rigid and he sensed I was going to go all feminist on him, he said, "El, it really is. You know it is. Guys don't get emotional about it like girls do." His hand rested between my neck and my shoulder and he smoothed his thumb back and forth over my skin.

I narrowed my eyes at him before asking the dumbest question ever. "So how many girls have you slept with, Jag?"

His thumb stopped its movement and he frowned then looked away, the muscles in his jaw jumping. "Does it matter?"

"No, I guess not," I mumbled, my heart taking a direct hit then. Why the hell had I even asked? Ugh. Now my imagination was gonna go wild thinking of who all he'd been with. Yay for me and my ridiculous questions.

"But, El, it's different with you and me… With you I *would* get emotional." He kissed me softly then rested his forehead against mine as he let that sink in.

And just like that, it was all better.

We only got to second base that night, and I was okay with that.

Chapter 7

I was seventeen when Jag broke my heart for the second time.

He'd finally decided that he'd play baseball at South Carolina University. Thirteen hours away. *Thirteen hours away!* I honestly didn't know how I'd survive being away from him or being that far from him. The only consolation in his choice was that he hadn't chosen Oregon State, which was thirty-two hours away. Although his being over half a day's drive away from me was bad enough, if he'd chosen O-State, that distance would've totally made me freak out. But I loved him and didn't want to stand in the way of his success, so I lied and told him that I was fine with everything and that I was so excited for him and hoped he did amazing. That kind of lying was okay, I told myself.

The day he signed his scholarship was crazy. The principal let all the classes go to the gym to watch and cheer him on. There was a table set up at center court for him and the head coaches of the high school team and the college team to sit at. His parents stood behind them, and it seemed as if every newspaper in the state had a sports writer there, their photographers clicking away like mad. His new college coach had given him a USC cap, which Jag had put on immediately with a huge smile.

I watched from the bleachers, standing by Rebecca, smiling with tears in my eyes, so proud of him and what he'd accomplished, when he suddenly looked up and around with a frown. Then he stood and scanned the crowd before spotting me and signaled for me to come down there. I shook my head stiffly, a little horrified that he'd want me with him. His mom then realized what he was doing and started nodding fervently at me, holding a hand out to me and wiggling her fingers as if to take mine from fifty feet away. Ugh. I ended up having no choice but to go as Rebecca pushed me in my back, nudging me to go to them. I gave her a dirty look before making my way through multiple students then stepping down onto the gym floor and walking to the table.

"Get in here, Ellen!" Mrs. Jensen cooed. "You're one of us, you know." Her smile made me smile. She had to be one of the nicest people I'd ever known.

So I stood there by Mrs. Jensen smiling like a fool wondering if the description in the picture would say, "Back row: Royce Jensen, father, Mary Jensen, mother, Ellen Love, hapless high school girlfriend who'll soon be dumped when Jagger Jensen goes off to college and discovers all the hot babes that await him in South Carolina." Great.

The day before Jag was to leave for college, we went to Tyler Callihan's official End of Summer Party. His family owned a private beach on Lake Michigan, so during the day we swam and then Tyler and a couple guys had taken some of us out on their family's boats. It was now evening, there was a bonfire blazing and the beer was flowing like crazy. Most of the senior class was there since it'd probably be the last time they'd be together for some time.

Jag and I had been hanging with Rebecca and Ross. We both wore hoodies over our swimsuits since it was always a little chilly on the lake at night, but I'd gotten too cold so we'd walked up to the house so I could get my yoga pants. Before going in the house, Jag pulled me around to the side of it for an impromptu make-out session where he pressed me against the house with his body as his lips covered mine. Wow. I didn't think I'd ever get enough of his kisses.

"God, El, you don't know what you do to me," he rasped in my ear after we'd kissed for a while.

I think I figured out pretty well what I did to him if what I felt against my stomach was any indication. We continued kissing as his hands slipped under my hoodie to the back to untie my bikini top at the bottom then they slid around to the front where he cupped my breasts and ran his thumbs over my nipples making me moan into his mouth.

"Jag… please…" I whispered as my fingers dug into his back under his hoodie.

Okay. I'd had enough. We'd had several hot and heavy stints that'd left me wanting him so badly I could hardly stand it. But Mr. Ultimate Gentleman always held back. Well, that was going to change tonight. I reached a hand around and down, stroking him over his swim trunks, eliciting a groan from his throat. He then placed his hand over mine, which was my "signal" to stop. Nope. Not happening this time. Still kissing him, I did something I'd never done before. I pulled my hand from his then found his waistband and plunged my hand inside his swim trunks, finding his shaft and grasping it firmly, moving it up and down his length. His head fell back on his shoulders as a growl rumbled from deep inside his chest. It was the most beautiful thing I'd ever seen.

"El…"

"Jag, let me make you feel good," I whispered.

Guess my speaking wasn't a wise choice. It was as if hearing my voice woke him up suddenly. His head came forward, his eyes focusing on mine, and a grimace appeared on his face as he reached inside his trunks grabbing my hand and pulling it away from him and out as he hissed, "Stop!"

Now I was pissed. I didn't understand. He'd had sex before, so why wouldn't he with me? "God! What's your problem, Jag? I'm all but throwing my fucking self at you but you want nothing to do with me!"

"You don't get it," he said quietly, trying not to draw attention to us.

No, I really didn't. "That's for damned sure! I guess I'm just not good enough for you, is that it, Jag? Oh, you can fuck all those other girls. But me?" I huffed out a sarcastic chuckle. "When it comes to me, no way!"

I wasn't deaf. It wasn't like I hadn't heard kids at school talking about who he'd been with, and there'd been several. Rebecca had even told me some of the locker room talk that Ross had let her in on. So why didn't Jag want me? I stood looking at him, hands on my hips waiting to see what he had to say.

He let out a frustrated breath and pushed that shock of dark hair out of his face. "Babe, it's just that you're, well, you're special."

I laughed at him then, shaking my head at how ridiculous he sounded, reaching my hands back to re-tie my bikini top. When his hands went to my shoulders, I moved my hands back around to his chest and shoved. He didn't budge which just pissed me off even more. "No, Jag. I'm tired of this. If you don't want me, then I don't see the point." I turned and walked back toward the bonfire, grabbing a beer from Nick Thomas on my way, not bothering to look back at Jag. Down by the lake, I looked around for Rebecca but she wasn't anywhere to be found. Damn it. I needed my best friend! I texted her and she responded that she and Ross were busy, so I let it go. They'd actually done the deed on Prom night and had been going at it steadily ever since. Whatever.

After an hour of hanging out with different people, Nick Thomas in particular who kept the beer coming, and watching Blair Adams, a girl Jag had dated and, according to my sources, slept with, and her current boyfriend, Josh Martin break up right in front of God and everyone, I realized I'd been a complete and utter tool for what I'd said to Jag. I needed to find him and apologize. I told Nick I'd be back then moving through the crowd, I asked around but no one had seen Jag. I made my way up to the house, a bit tipsy from all the beer that Nick had kept supplying me with. Inside, no one had seen Jag either, so I went out front to see if his

Camaro was still there, which it was, so I went back inside to find him.

Still not seeing him, I went upstairs to use the restroom. When I finished, I decided to get my yoga pants because I was so freaking cold from being down by the beach for the past hour. Jag had put our bags in one of the bedrooms, so I went to the first one but the door was locked. The second room was empty, so I moved to the last. The door was cracked and I peeked in, and there sat Jag on the bed with his back to me, his arm around Blair Adams' shoulders, hers around his waist.

I froze and my heart leaped into my throat almost choking me. What the hell? When Blair leaned over and kissed him, I unfroze and literally charged into the room.

"What the fuck?" I shrieked.

I'd never seen two people jump up so fast in my life.

"El!" Was that guilt all over Jag's face? Oh God.

I was proud of myself for not bursting into tears. Instead, I huffed as I nodded slowly. "I see." It was all I could say. And it all became so clear just then. It wasn't that Jag didn't want to sleep with me because I was special. It was because he'd wanted Blair all along. And now that she and Josh had broken up, Jag hadn't wasted any time moving in to claim her back. I turned and ran from the room, hearing him yell after me, then flew down the stairs looking around for someone, anyone, to get me the fuck out of there. Pushing through the crowd, I saw Nick Thomas, so Nick it was.

"I need to go *now*!" I hissed, grabbing him by the arm and dragging him to the front door with me.

"I'm on it!" he said, digging his keys from his shorts pocket while I pulled him out the door.

"El, wait!" Jag yelled, coming after us.

I knew it'd take some time for him to get through everyone as big as he was, but I wasn't taking any chances as I told Nick to hurry. We got to his car, and I jumped inside locking the door. After Nick got in and started the car, Jag ran up to my window putting his hands on the glass.

"El, get out!" he yelled, but I just stared straight ahead ignoring him. "El!"

"Go!" I told Nick and we took off. There was a loud sound, so I assumed Jag had hit the trunk with his fists as we drove off.

"What the fuck?" Nick spat. "This is a goddamned Lexus, for Christ's sake! Fucker better not have dented it!"

"I'll pay for it if there are any damages. God," I clipped out. Jeez. Guys and their cars.

We drove in silence for a few minutes before Nick broke it. "So what happened with you two?"

I really didn't want to get into it, but I was pissed so I told him anyway. "I caught him in a bedroom with Blair Adams."

He nodded as if he totally understood that crazy bit of info then looked over at me and so kindly contributed, "Yeah, I heard they fucked like goddamned rabbits when they dated. I was kinda surprised when he broke it off with her. I mean, look at her. Chick's fucking stacked." He looked over at me again realizing what he'd said and tried consoling me. "I mean, you're hot and all too, don't get me wrong."

"Yeah. Thanks for that, Nick. Appreciate it." I scowled back at him then faced the front again with a heavy sigh.

"Isn't Jag leaving for South Carolina tomorrow anyway? He's gonna be pretty far away. Wouldn't make sense for you to keep dating, would it?"

Captain Tactful was about to get on my last nerve. "No, probably not."

"So, would you wanna go out with me sometime?"

Uh, hell to the no. "Um, I don't know. We'll see."

I couldn't believe I still wasn't crying. Maybe the beer had dehydrated me and I didn't have any to shed. Maybe I was in shock. I don't know what it was, but I was actually thankful that I wasn't a blubbering mess with Nick trying to comfort me. God knew he wasn't the most empathetic person to be around. He yammered on and on the rest of the way to my house about how he was only taking one semester at Northwestern before he interned at his dad's business—in my dazed state I hadn't even caught what type of business it was—and how he'd take over someday and probably be a millionaire and didn't I want to go out with someone who had such a stellar future.

That would be a big, fat negative.

When we pulled into my drive I thought I was going to cry just being free from all the blathering.

"Thanks, Nick. I appreciate it a lot." I opened the car door and started to get out.

"Hey, no problem. Can I get your number?"

Just as I was going to tell him that my family didn't believe in phones, a car came screeching around the corner. Make that a dusk blue '69 Camaro came screeching around the corner, pulling up and skidding to a stop right in front of my house. Jag got out, slamming his door loudly and stalked toward me, his eyes glittering with anger.

Whoa.

"Hey, thanks again, Nick. Uh, see you around," I said and shut the car door, turning to go inside the house.

"El!" Jag bellowed from behind me.

I stopped and turned around, glaring at him. Then my glare went to Nick who still sat in my drive wanting to see the show, I guessed. I waved at him and he finally got the hint, waving back then pulling out to leave.

Jag was there then. "El, let me explain."

I looked up at him, not able to keep the hurt from my eyes. He took a step toward me and I took one back.

"El..."

And that's when the tears came. Damn it.

"El, I'm so sorry. Please, let me explain things to you."

I couldn't stop crying long enough to speak. He was on his own here.

"Will you come sit in the car with me?" he asked.

I nodded, crossing my arms over my chest as I continued crying, and followed him to his car. He opened the passenger door for me and I slid inside, but I started crying even harder when I thought that this could be the last time I'd ever be inside the damned thing.

When he got in, he started it. "Ride with me?" he asked, looking over at me.

All I could do was nod again, the lump in my throat keeping me from talking. He didn't talk either as we drove. We ended up at his thinking place, which kept my tears coming, since I realized we might not ever go there together again. Despite the lump in my throat, I wanted to scream. Wanted to throw a fit and ask him what the hell was going on, but I remained silent as we stared out at the city below us, the tears silently flowing down my face.

He cleared his throat then said, "What happened tonight isn't what you thought it was, El."

I lowered my head, looking down at my hands in my lap, wondering how it could've been anything else.

He reached over and lifted my chin with his finger, turning me to face him. The look on his face gutted me; he was so distraught and unsure of himself. "El, what you saw was nothing. I went in the room to get your pants for you figuring you'd probably be cold, but before I could, Blair came in. She was upset and crying and told me what'd happened with her and Josh. We sat down and talked about it for a bit. She was really torn up. Hell, I wasn't much better, wondering if you were going to break up with me."

I frowned at that. He really thought I was going to break up with him?

"What you saw was, well, I guess she was just thanking me for listening. I mean, I didn't kiss her back, if that's what you were wondering." He looked at me as if he were trying to find forgiveness in my eyes, but there really wasn't any there. I knew what I'd seen.

"But you had your arm around her," I mumbled.

"In a big brother kind of way."

"When I saw you, it all became clear to me, Jag. I couldn't understand why you don't want me, and then I realized it was because you want her," I said, my stupid tears starting to fall harder.

"El..." His hand went behind my neck and he pulled me closer to rest his forehead against mine. "I want you. I want you all the fucking time. God, you drive me wild. But at first, I just thought you were too young, and as things have progressed, I didn't want this to just be about sex. Not with you. Never with you." He touched his lips to mine. "You mean so much more to me, babe."

This made sense to me in a way, yet it didn't. "I still don't get it, Jag. I want you to be my first. I want you to be my only. I honestly don't understand what's holding you back."

He sighed, now cupping my face with both hands and wiping my tears away with his thumbs. "It's because it's you."

I pulled back and looked at him with a scowl. Well, that wasn't very nice.

He chuckled a little, continuing to hold my face in his hands. "I mean, it's *you*, El. It'd be a huge step. You've always been a part of my life." At my raised eyebrow, he repeated, "Always. Even when you thought I didn't care about you, when we didn't hang out for all those years, I always cared. Always kept an eye out for you. If something happened now where we didn't work out, it'd break me. I can't even think about us not being together. And I don't want you to ever *not* be in my life. I know that's really selfish of me, isn't it? But does it make any sense to you?" He kissed me again softly.

"Yeah, it *is* selfish of you." I had to agree with him on that one.

He sighed. "I know."

"But that's just being scared, Jag. Relationships are a risk. Nothing's guaranteed."

"You're right," he conceded, letting my face go and sitting back in his seat and staring straight ahead. "I *am* scared. Scared of my feelings for you. Scared of how things are going to be once I leave."

"I'm scared too. And I guess I get what you're saying, but then again I don't," I whispered. "Because you're scared of losing me, you don't want to be with me. Right?" We sat there in silence for a bit. "So it'd be okay if I was with someone else?"

Well, that was the wrong thing to say. His head jerked toward me so fast I almost felt the air stir from his abrupt movement, and the mood in the car had changed suddenly, thick with his fury. He grabbed me by the shoulders, pulling me toward him. When his angry face was an inch from mine he hissed out, "No, it is *not* goddamned okay for you to be with someone else!"

I was so confused. He wanted me but he didn't want me. And he didn't want anyone else to have me. Oooookay.

He let go of my shoulders and ran a hand over his face then looked at me and said, "El, I'm sorry. That wasn't fair. Look, when we started this up, I wanted to take it slow. Get to know each other again." He looked down at his lap. "Then when I realized I was in love with you, I knew I'd be leaving soon, and I didn't want to do this to you... sleep with you then just up and leave." He looked at me again, confusion in his eyes. "God, I don't know how to explain it. It made sense in my fucking head at the time. I just know... I won't ask you to wait for me." He closed his eyes and took a deep breath blowing it out slowly.

I sat looking at him knowing what I'd do even if he was right that it wasn't fair to me. I loved him, so I was willing to wait for him. However long that may be.

Chapter 8

I was nineteen when I decided to branch out a little.

"Jag!" I semi yelled. He'd fallen asleep again while we were on the phone. When I couldn't get him to wake up, I hung up with a sigh knowing we'd probably talk the next night. If he wasn't too tired, that was. Poor guy was run ragged with all the games he'd been playing on top of the classes he was taking.

The past two and a half years had been, well, interesting. Jag had been very successful pitching up a damned storm, much to the thrill of his coaches, and his team had advanced to the finals of the College World Series both years, which meant they'd played clear to the end of June, meaning I only got to see him over the summer for a few weeks. Of course I saw him at Thanksgiving and Christmas, but again only for a week or so each time. But I'd gotten to go see him play in a few games, and I'd even watched him play on ESPN a couple times. The games I'd seen him play in person were when my family had driven down to South Carolina over spring break my junior year and when I'd gone to Omaha with Jag's family for the CWS finals the past two years.

Our visits were pretty fleeting and hectic since his team usually played the visiting team three games in a row, so he didn't have much time to be with me. But it was all good. Our relationship had actually heated up more when we did get together. We'd actually made it to third base a couple times, which was a step in the right direction, I thought. Not that I was obsessed with having sex with him or anything. It was just that there was that slightest nagging always in the back of my head leaving me to wonder about what he'd told me, wondering if he was really just protecting me by not sleeping with me or if he was just keeping me sidelined from being with anyone else. Or if he loved me but not in *that way*. Or if he was really, seriously scared of going there with me and then we didn't work out.

Chick Think I called what I was doing, and it pissed me off because whenever I allowed myself to go there, it was exhausting.

Rebecca had thought it was sweet what Jag had said, telling me that good things come to those who wait, to which I'd snarkily replied that *coming* comes to those who don't, which made her laugh.

But Jag and I talked or texted almost every day when we were apart and also sent cards and silly stuff to each other regularly. In the spirit of, well, school spirit, I'd sent him a penis-shaped pillow as a mascot and he'd sent me a bumper sticker that said "I Love 'Cocks" which, after several arguments, I finally succumbed to Dad's refusal of letting me put it on my car.

I'd finally graduated high school and planned on attending Northwestern in the fall. I'd taken concurrent courses my senior year, so I'd knocked out several of the basics and was well on my way to getting into the physical therapy program by my junior year. Rebecca wanted to be a nurse anesthetist, so we'd both be taking several of the same science classes when it came to our degrees.

First semester, we drove to our classes together since we both lived at home, but after we'd proven with our grades that we were serious about this college stuff, our parents let us get an apartment together, and it was awesome! We felt so grown up. We both got jobs at the Starbucks in Norris Center, so at least we were trying to help our parents out with the bills some.

Jag had been excited for me though he hadn't gotten to see my new place, but I'd emailed him gobs of pictures of it. I quickly found that living in the apartment made me miss him even more because Rebecca and Ross were still dating which meant Ross spent the night regularly. He was attending Northwestern also and majoring in criminal justice. So I had to deal with watching them being all lovey-dovey while my celibate, virgin self pined for my boyfriend. Good times.

"El! We're going to the party at Slade's house tonight. Come with us!" Rebecca called from her bedroom.

So Slade Ryan was holding another party, eh? Hm. Slade was a guy we worked with at Starbuck's who was our age and also attended Northwestern. Rebecca and I had decided that he was forbidden fruit. He was just too damned cute with his surfer-boy look, shaggy blond hair, tanned skin and gorgeous green eyes. Oh, and when he smiled, the dimples in his cheeks were like an inch deep showing off his perfectly straight, white teeth. See? Totally cute. And talk about a flirt. The guy had to hold the Guinness record for most hours of nonstop flirting ever.

"Can't. Jag's gonna be calling soon," I hollered back from where I sat on the sofa watching TV.

I heard her growl and spit out a few choice words, informing me under her breath that it was a Friday night and it shouldn't be wasted in front of the TV, all of which I ignored.

Rebecca was worried about me. I stayed in almost every night waiting for Jag to call. Therefore, she and I went through the same routine over and over:

Come out with us, El!

Can't. Jag's gonna call.

You can go one night without talking to him.

I know, but I don't want to.

You think he's not going out down there? That he's being a good little boyfriend?

blank stare

I'm sorry, El. I wasn't trying to hurt your feelings. I just want you to have a life outside of Jag.

I do have a life.

snort Yeah, in class, at work or hanging at home waiting for him to call. You're always waiting.

Just because I don't go out and drink copious amounts of adult beverages doesn't mean I don't have a life. *scowl*

eye roll Whatever.

And round and round it went.

At least I got a lot of studying done. Whoopee.

So after Rebecca and Ross left, I waited for Jag to call. And waited. And waited. And then waited some more. I knew he didn't have a game that night or any over the weekend, so that couldn't have been what was holding him up. By ten o'clock, I'd had it with the waiting and called him.

"Hello. You've reached the very sexy Jagger Jensen's phone," answered a sultry female voice. "How can I help you?"

I was a little stunned to say the least. I could hear the sounds of a party going on in the background. Thank God it wasn't quiet which would've led me to believe that Jag was alone with this chick. "Is Jag around?"

"And who may I say is calling?" the deeply accented voice asked.

Ah. A real live Southern belle. And all I could think of at that moment was Prissy screaming in her baby voice, "I don't know nothin' 'bout birthin' babies!" for some stupid ass reason. Ugh. Memory retention. It's a fine thing.

"Tell him it's Ellen."

"Helen?" she said in a smooth, snarky drawl.

I knew she'd heard my name correctly, had probably seen it on his caller ID before she'd answered. Whatever. "Ellen. Ellen Love."

"Oh. Ellen? Well, Jag's never mentioned having a friend named Ellen. Let me see if he wants to take your call. I was using his phone to make my own call when you interrupted," her sweeter-than-pie voice dragged out.

It took everything I had not to answer, "Frankly, my dear, I don't give a damn." I mean, how many times in life do you get to even use that line much less have it set up so perfectly? Sad thing was, Ms. Magnolia probably wouldn't have cottoned on to what I'd done there, so better to withhold than to waste a golden opportunity on an idiot, I always say.

Now, I didn't think Jag would cheat on me. And if he *were* going to cheat, I didn't think it'd be that blatant, so in my face. So Little Ms. Thang, whoever she was, had just happened to get his phone and I'd called at just the right time. It happened. Nothing to beat her face in about. This time. I snorted to myself at this lovely thought.

"Hello?" I heard Jag yell into the phone.

"Yeah. What's up?"

"El? Hang on. I can't hear you."

I heard the music getting quieter as he moved from wherever the party was. I heard him fumbling around with the phone before he asked again, "El?"

"Yeah." Now, I said I didn't think he'd cheat on me. I didn't say it didn't piss me off that some little twerp was answering his phone.

"What's going on?"

"I was wondering the same," I said, deadpan.

"Sorry about that. Wendy's kind of…"

"A bitch?"

He chuckled. "Yeah, you could say that. I'm sorry. She asked to use my phone to call her boyfriend when you called."

"Where are you?" I asked.

"Just at Doug and Jason's apartment. What're you doing?"

"Well, I could be out partying myself, but I decided to stay home and wait for your call."

"Partying? Where?" he asked with an edge to his voice.

Oh, no. Uh uh. He did *not* get to go all possessive on me after what'd just occurred. "Just to a party with Rebecca and Ross. It's not like I'd be hanging around some guy and loaning my phone out to him so he'd answer it if you happened to call…"

"El, I didn't plan it that way. I was going to call you later. It's Friday, so I didn't think you'd go to bed until after midnight."

"What'd you think I'd be doing, Jag?" I sighed. "God, Rebecca's right. I *don't* have a life. Sometimes I feel like all I do is sit around and wait for you to call."

"We've talked about this before, El. I don't expect you to wait around. Go do things. Hang out with your friends. *Have* a life!"

So, Mr. Possessive Alpha Male was telling me this after he'd just about bitten my head off when I told him about a party?

"Do you ever get tired of it, Jag?"

He sighed. "Tired of what, El?" He knew what I was going to say.

"Just… being apart." It'd been almost three months since we'd seen each other at Christmas.

He was quiet for a few beats. "Yeah, I get tired of it. I want you here with me. I want to be with you, El, but we both know that's not gonna happen right now. We've got a lot going on. Why? Are you getting tired of it?"

I sighed now. I *was* tired of it. I wanted him here with me. Home. Away from Wendy and her Ya-Ya Sisterhood crew. But it wasn't Jag's fault. It was no one's fault. It was just life. "No. I mean, yeah, I'm tired of not seeing you, of course. I'm tired of random chicks answering your phone."

"That happened once," he scoffed.

"And if it happens again?"

"Not gonna happen again. Trust, El. We've got to trust each other."

"Yeah. So if I went ahead and went to a party with Rebecca and Ross tonight, would you trust me?"

I could hear him take a deep breath then let it out. "El, it's not that I don't trust *you*. It's all those horny bastards who'd be checking you out that I don't trust."

"Oh, so *you* can go out, but I should stay home and just learn to deal with all the horny bitches wanting a piece of you then, right? That's what you're saying?"

"I don't wanna fight, El."

"Who's fighting, Jag?" My voice level had increased and my blood pressure was spiking, I was sure, but who was fighting?

"Well, this isn't exactly not fighting," he said with a chuckle.

"I'm sorry. It just pisses me off sometimes, hell all the time, that we're apart. And it doesn't help seeing Rebecca and Ross together day in and day out. It's just not fair."

"I know, babe, but there's nothing we can do about it right now. I'm sorry."

It was my turn to take a deep breath and release it. "I know. I'm sorry too."

We sat there being silent together.

"El?"

"Yeah?"

"If it helps, I love you. Forever and a day."

And leave it to him to turn things around. "I love you too, Jag. Always," I whispered.

We hung up having made it over that little snag. But I'd made up my mind that I *was* going to start living my life more, stop waiting around, and have fun. Because Rebecca had told me I wasn't. And because Jag told me I should. I went to my bathroom and dug through my makeup.

"Okay, going for dramatic tonight," I declared.

After making my eyes smoky, I poufed my hair big. Not bad. I was ecstatic to see that I wasn't totally helpless in the looking like a girl department.

I headed to my bedroom and looked through my closet, finding some nice jeans and a cute little navy, peplum blouse with a back zip to wear, pairing that with Rebecca's five-inch sparkly navy heels and I was good to go.

Chapter 9

I was still nineteen when I when I got a taste of the party life on my own.

I arrived at Slade's party looking pretty good, if I did say so myself. It was nice to dress up for a change in the evening instead of resorting to baggy sweatpants and an old t-shirt while I waited around for Jag to call. When Rebecca saw me, she all but pounced on me.

"El! Oh my God! I'm so glad you're here!" she squealed hugging me.

My teeth clacked in my head as she jumped up and down clinging to me. "Um, how about you calm down now?" I said with a snort putting my hands on her shoulders to keep her still.

"But we haven't gone out together in forever! I'm just so happy to see you here!" she said beaming at me.

If that's all it took to make my bestie happy, then I was good with it. I put a finger on the rim of her cup tilting it down to peek inside it. "What's your poison?"

"Rocket Fuel."

"Bec." I raised an eyebrow at her.

"El." She snickered, giving me the same look.

The last time she'd gone to a party at Slade's, she'd come home with Ross so drunk she could hardly walk. Apparently, this Rocket Fuel was a concoction that was made up of beer, lemonade and vodka with a bit of Everclear thrown in for good measure that was meant to knock you on your ass, which she'd proven loud and clear. Loud because listening to her that night puking in the bathroom had been awesome (not), and clear because the whole next day she'd looked like hammered shit.

"I'll pass."

"No! You have to try it!"

I narrowed my eyes at her as she shoved her cup in my face. But when I took a sip, it actually was pretty good. I raised my eyebrows and puckered out my lips making my assessment. "Not bad."

"Told you! Let's go get you a cup."

We wended our way through the gobs of people to the screen-enclosed back porch where there was, swear to God, what looked like a freaking horse tank full of the drink. I slowly turned my head and looked at Rebecca all *You've* got *to be shitting me.* She giggled and grabbed a cup for me, dipping it into the pool of liquor. Wow.

"Is this even sanitary?" I asked.

"This batch is. Last party, some guy was so messed up that I guess he took a piss in it."

My face blanched and I pulled my cup away from my lips. "Uh."

Rebecca laughed. "Just drink it, El. I watched them make it. It's cool."

"Still can't be too clean with people dipping their cups in, you know. I mean, it's kinda like double dipping and that's just gross. Ew, and what if their nasty fingers get all in it?"

Rebecca gave me a look. "El, it's alcohol not friggin' holy water. Drink."

So I did, trying not to think about everyone's and their dog's germs floating around in the damned pool, hoping that the Everclear would at least kill some of the germs. I downed what was in my cup quickly, hoping it'd take effect and I'd stop worrying about all the various diseases I could be contracting.

We walked over to where Ross was talking to some guys who'd gone to our high school and when they saw me, all of them wanted to know how Jag was doing. I told them that his team was flying to Texas for three conference games the next week when all of a sudden I was picked up from behind, twirled around and mugged by a pair of lips on my neck.

"Baby doll!" Slade said as he set me down, spinning me to him, a huge grin on his face as he looked down at me.

"Hey Slade!" I grinned back. God, he was too cute.

He leaned down to put his forehead on mine, wrapping his arms around my waist. "'Bout time you came to one of my soirees."

Now, if I'd been observant, I'd have noticed the four or five cameras that'd come out to gather evidence. But as it was, I was completely oblivious, the liquor already taking effect and the charisma that all but gushed from Slade overtaking me. "Soiree, huh? Pretty fancy title for a place where people ladle their libations from a lagoon," I pulled back and said.

Slade threw his head back and laughed then looked down at me, eyes twinkling. "God, you're adorable. When are you gonna go out with me?"

I laughed. "When you quit trying so hard." I smirked up at him.

He nodded as if seriously taking that in making me roll my eyes. "You're empty," he said looking in my cup. "Let's go partake from the pond, shall we?" he said with a snort then laced an arm around my shoulders and led me away.

Slade was particularly charming and kept me entertained for most of the night with his crazy sense of humor and his constant attention, and I had to admit, although a little guiltily, that it was nice being the object of someone's attention for a change.

At the end of the night, we sat on the back porch in a swing. "El, let's make a toast," he said.

"To what?" I asked with a drunken snort.

"To us." He clinked his cup against mine.

"Uh, to us," I echoed then drank, at that point not giving one shit whether I'd wake up with hand, foot and mouth disease from consuming from the communal cauldron.

"So why haven't we ever gotten together?" he asked.

"Maybe because I have a boyfriend?"

"Oh. That. Well, he's not here now…"

"Slade…"

"Oh, lighten up, El. You only live once, you know."

"Yeah, and I'm definitely putting that to the test by drinking this shit." I held up my cup giving a nod toward it.

He laughed. "Gotta live dangerously too."

"And this is proof positive that I'm doing just that," I said laughing with him.

"So, who is this guy again? Rebecca has told me a little about him."

"Jag Jensen. We've been best friends since I was five and he was seven."

"Daaaaaang, that's a long time to know someone."

I nodded agreeing with him that it *was* a long time.

"So what are the chances that you'd ever leave his ass behind and go out with me?" He looked at me, sporting that cute smile, dimples and all, which just about knocked me out of the swing, his green eyes glittering in the moonlight.

I chuckled. "I'd have to say slim to none." I was in love with Jag. It wasn't like some cute beach boy was going to change that anytime too soon.

He nodded as he looked at me, his eyes burning into mine as he smoothed a piece of my hair off my face. Whoa. This was getting a little too serious. "So you're saying there's a chance?" He then grinned at his movie line quote, his serious look a faded memory. Thank God.

I almost did a spit take at that, having been caught up in the seriousness for a second or two. I should've known Slade would make things silly again like he always did. It was definitely part of his appeal. We laughed then quoted more of the movie lines like the drunken idiots that we were.

When the party ended, Ross wouldn't let me drive home, so he rounded up Rebecca and me, enduring our giggling fits, and piled us into his old Bronco, mumbling something about Rebecca being the designated driver the next three parties, that putting up with this shit made her owe him big time, which made us laugh even harder.

"That was fun!" I said from the back seat.

"See? I told you!" Rebecca said from the front. "What were you and Slide up to?"

I burst out laughing. "Slide?"

She turned to look at me, her forehead wrinkling. "Glide."

I fell over on the seat laughing, snorting out, "Glide?"

"What am I trying to say?" she asked looking helplessly at Ross.

"Slade," he answered with a roll of his eyes.

"Yes! Glade!" Even Ross couldn't help but cracking up at her then.

I'd never laughed so hard in my life. I'd definitely been missing out on the good times by not going to parties with Rebecca that was for sure. But I also knew I'd missed out by not just hanging out with her or my other friends, which I resolved to change.

When we got to our apartment, I stumbled out of Ross's vehicle and staggered inside, not waiting for them, needing to get to my bed and lie down. I fell face-first onto it and felt the world spinning for a while before passing out.

Chapter 10

And I was still nineteen when I pissed Jag off but good.

I felt so hot. Why was it so hot in the apartment? Had Rebecca turned up the heat? And, ouch, damn it. My head felt like a frickin' Slayer song had set up residence inside it, the tune banging so damned hard against my skull that it made me want to cry. Stupid Rocket Fuel. Now I remembered why I didn't go with Rebecca to those stupid parties—the mornings after. But, God, now I was sweating like crazy and I didn't know why.

I realized that I'd somehow gotten under the covers of my bed and I was still clothed. Oh. That was why I was so hot. Keeping my eyes closed so the sun coming in my window didn't make the pounding in my head worse, I unzipped my jeans, yanking them off and throwing them outside the covers. I then unzipped my blouse, pulling it over my head and sending it the same direction as my jeans, which left me in my bra and panties. Ah, that was better.

But after a few minutes, I realized that it wasn't better. I was still freaking burning up. And then it hit me. Oh, God! Maybe I really *had* contracted hand, foot and mouth disease! I groaned, thinking that I'd have to miss class the next week, I'd have to make arrangements for someone to work for me, I'd have to let Slade know to call all the people who'd drunk of the miserable mixture, when suddenly the source of all the damned heat I was feeling made itself known to me. From behind me, an arm wound its way over my panty-clad hip then curled down to between my legs, where the hand splayed against me then cupped me, pulling me tighter into the body of its owner.

Oh, shit. Had Slade come home with me and he was now in my bed? My body went still as I lay there thinking how in the world that'd happened and how the hell was I going to get out of this one. His head moved to the back of my neck, his hot breath on me making me shiver as his lips grazed over my skin. Oh, God, that felt really good as did his fingers gliding over me. When he pulled me even closer, I felt his erection against my butt, which made me tense up, but as I tried moving away, I pretty much ground my ass against the damned thing, which made him moan.

Shit! Shit, shit, shit!

This was so not good. Okay, I needed to stop this now before things got even worse. And to think I'd thought my damned hangover was my biggest problem right then. Lord.

"Slade?" I whispered. His lips on my neck froze, his fingers below stopping their amazing exploration since I'd put my hand down there to stop him, and I felt his body become rigid. "Slade, what are you do—" I started as I slowly turned over to face him.

And imagine my motherfricking shock when I saw Jag's intense glacier blue eyes piercing mine.

"Slade?" he asked, sitting up, scowling down at me. "Is that the guy you were hanging all over last night?"

"Jag? Wha—? How'd you—? When did you—?" Guess I needed to take another English course next semester, huh? Holy shit! Why was he here? How'd he get here? I lay there staring at him trying to get my wits about me wondering if I was just drunk and imagining this all. I closed my eyes tightly then tried again. Yep. He was still sitting there glaring down at me. And he was in my bed. Wearing nothing but his boxer briefs.

Wait.

Jag was sitting in my bed wearing nothing but his boxer briefs!

And he was sporting a pretty massive boner. Oh my God!

My head spun for a few minutes and I threw my forearm over my eyes, letting this all soak in as I let out a groan. How the hell was this happening? There was a heavy silence and then I felt the bed shifting as he got up. I next heard him pulling on his jeans. Shit.

In my semi-drunken confusion all I could do was lie there waiting on the pink elephants to start marching in and trumpeting away. Was this really happening?

"El? El, take this," he said after a few moments, pulling my arm away from my face. I opened my eyes and looked up at him. He was holding out a glass of water and had two aspirins in his other hand toward me. Yep. This was definitely happening. I carefully pushed myself to sit up.

"Thanks." I took the pills and the glass and downed them both, as I silently vowed to never drink again. Too many weird things happened. And the mornings after were oh so much fun too, what with the pounding head and, oh, yeah, the boyfriend who'd been eight-hundred miles away showing up out of the blue. Just. Awesome.

I leaned over to set the glass on my bedside table then moved back and closing my eyes, rested back against the wall, thankful that Mom had made me leave my bed with the iron frame at home, even though I'd begged her to let me take it. It just would've hurt my back now anyway. After a few seconds, I became coherent enough to speak. "How did you get here?" I asked in a gravelly voice, looking up at him then looked over at my clock to see that it was after one in the afternoon. Yeesh.

He stood by my bed, arms crossed over his chest watching me. He was way angry, his eyes navy (which I knew meant that he was either really turned on or just majorly *majorly* pissed. Um, I was going to go with *majorly* pissed at that point), boring into mine. That hunk of dark hair hung over them making me want to reach up and push it away. He still hadn't put his shirt on and I couldn't keep my eyes from roaming over his hard, sculpted chest, his biceps bulging from his fists clenched under them, or the ripped plane of his abs that led to the defined V that disappeared down inside his unbuttoned jeans. Damn. He blew out a breath then said, "When the guys started sending me all the pictures of you hanging on that guy, I got pretty pissed. I tried calling you, but you didn't answer your phone. What was going on there, El?"

Busted.

My five-year-old self came out in that moment, immediately pointing its accusing finger at someone else. "It wasn't my fault, Jag! I wasn't the one hanging on Slade. He was hanging on me!" And sharing that angle with him went over great. His eyes dared me to say more. Nope, not happening. I wasn't dumb enough to provoke him further as I watched the muscles in his jaws jumping as he took in what I'd said.

"Go take a shower and we'll talk after," was all he said as he took in a deep breath and blew it out. Two deep breaths in less than five minutes. Yep. He was pissed.

Ooookay. I got out of bed, shuffling like an eighty-year-old woman to the door, my body and brain still reeling from the enervating effects of fucking Rocket Fuel.

I wasn't self conscious about being just in my bra and panties because Jag had seen me in my swimsuit a million times before, which was about the same as what I had on. Before leaving the room, I turned to look at him just to make sure he was really there. He was. And the way he was looking me up and down right then was a total turn on. If I hadn't felt so awful, I'd probably have jumped on him, but as it was, I felt like crap, so I passed for now.

And what good would it have done anyway, I thought, as I left my room. We'd never had sex and I'd begun to think we never would. But Jag *had* behaved pretty friskily right before I'd turned over thinking he was Slade, so maybe there was a chance. A slim chance since we were going to discuss what'd happened last night and this morning after I showered, but still, there was a chance.

And thinking that reminded me of Slade and our *Dumb and Dumber* quoting contest which made me snicker then frown. Nothing like thinking about one boy while another's in your room.

But I loved the boy in my room. And what had happened this morning should've proven it to him because I wasn't going to cheat. I just hoped he saw it that way.

Chapter 11

I was almost twenty when I lost my soul to Jag.

After showering, I felt immensely better, something about the water splashing down being a sort of baptism, a cleansing away of all the grime that clung to me both mentally and physically. I came out of the bathroom in nothing but a towel, my dark, wet hair hanging down my back, rivulets of water running from the ends only to be absorbed into the towel.

Rebecca met me in the hallway. "El!" she whisper-hissed, grabbing my hand and pulling me back inside the bathroom and closing the door. "Oh my God! Ross said Jag is here?" She looked almost crazed.

I just nodded.

"Why?" she asked in a shrill whisper.

"He said he was sent pictures of me with Slade last night," I explained with a groan.

"Shit!"

No duh, shit. More like double shit. Hell, triple shit would suffice in this situation because all along I'd been silently freaking out inside since I'd turned to see him in my bed. "Jag was in my bed when I woke up!" I whispered back.

"What?" Her eyes got great big.

"In his boxer briefs!" I added.

I thought her eyes were going to bug out of her head when she heard that. I had to reach over and use my fingers to close her mouth.

"Do you think you're finally going to…"

"I don't know! This is just crazy!"

She nodded thoughtfully. "Do you want Ross and me to leave? We could go to his place, even though it's kinda smelly because Joe doesn't know how to clean up after himself, damned pig."

I bit my bottom lip. *Did* I want them to leave? Did I really want to be alone with Jag right now as angry as he was? We did need to talk. "Yeah, if you don't mind. I mean, if you're good with it."

She waggled her eyebrows at me. "Oh, I'm good with it." She snorted and grabbed my wet shoulders. "El, it's time!" she squealed quietly.

I smiled weakly at her.

"El, it'll be fine. It's Jag. He'll be sweet to you. Believe me, once you get past that initial burn, it's all good, okay? Promise." She raised her eyebrows, nodding again at me.

Ugh. My best friend was coaching me on how to have sex. Yay.

"I'm gonna go get dressed and then we're outta here. Call me when you're done so we can discuss the dirty details!" She was so excited I couldn't help but huff out a laugh at her.

"God, Bec, calm down. It's kinda weird that you're like my cherry's personal cheerleader. And you're making me really nervous now," I muttered.

"It'll be fine, El! Okay, we're outta here! Don't forget to call me! I know Ross wants to hang out with Jag before he leaves." She squeezed my hand then left to go to her room.

I looked at myself in the mirror one last time then took a deep breath before going to my room.

When I opened the door, I saw Jag sitting at the foot of my bed, elbows on his knees and his forehead in the heels of his hands. Crap. That was the pose of someone who was trying to get a handle on things in a calm manner, key word being *trying*. Shit was about to get real and someone was going to get chewed plum out. Uh, namely, me.

"Jag?" I whispered softly as I closed my door quietly.

He sat up, running his hands over his face. When he finally looked at me, his eyes went dark as he saw me standing there in my towel. "C'mere."

I slowly walked over to him. His hands came out and landed on my hips and his head went down to where the top of it rested against my stomach. I remembered he'd done the same thing on Prom night. I ran my fingers through his hair as he stayed that way for a while before he looked up at me. "Do you want that guy? Slade?"

I frowned down at him, moving my hands to rest on his broad shoulders. "No. Of course not. You're the only one I've ever wanted, Jag."

He breathed out a shaky breath and pulled me down to sit sideways on his lap. "You're the only one for me too." His hand went to the back of my neck and he drew me closer, his other hand clutching my hip, arm across my thighs. "I want you, El," he said looking at me with his dark eyes before pressing his lips against mine, kissing me deep and wet and hard, not giving me any mixed messages at all as to what he meant.

He wanted me. He finally wanted me.

And now I was confused.

I pulled away from him, a little suspicious. "Why now, Jag?" I asked, my brow wrinkled trying not to be hurt if he was pulling some alpha male jealous bullshit here. "Is it because of Slade?"

He looked at me for a few seconds, moving his hand on my hip over to take my hand. He looked down watching as his long fingers played a phantom song using my fingers as the guitar strings. Then he sighed and looked up at me. "No, it's not because of him. I mean, seeing you with him in those pictures kind of woke me up." He looked at me and his face got serious. "Shit, El, I'm almost twenty-fucking-two and I want to finally make love to my girlfriend." His eyes roamed my face as he tried to gauge my reaction to that. I think he liked what he saw because he smiled and touched his lips to mine.

Then he grimaced a little and continued. "I know you probably think I've been an asshole for not being with you, but I was only protecting you. You were so young and innocent... and time, well, it's just slipped by. And when we've been together lately, it's so short, I didn't want you to think I'm just wanting in your pants. God, I guess that just sounds ridiculous, huh?" He now looked disgusted with himself as he ran his hand through his hair, moving that unruly, albeit persevering, shock out of his face.

"We're here now and we have time," I said, cupping his jaw as I leaned in and touched his lips with mine. "And I kinda want you in my pants... even though I'm not wearing any."

His eyes went molten and he turned and laid me back on the bed, moving over me to kiss me deeply, his hand tugging at my towel, throwing it across the room, and my arms wrapped around his back, my fingers digging into the hard muscle. God, I wanted him too, more than anything.

He pulled away, leaning on his elbow, to look at me. I was first panting from his kiss, and then from watching him look at me, which made my heart pound hard inside my chest. He'd never seen me fully naked before and I wasn't sure what he'd think. I felt his eyes roaming over my body, assessing what he saw and I wanted to cover myself from his penetrating gaze until his beautiful eyes rose to meet mine, burning hot, and he lightly cupped my jaw and rasped out, "You're beautiful, El."

He leisurely ran his hand from my jaw down between my breasts then to my stomach making my breathing speed up. His eyes had followed the path of his hand and as he kept moving it lower, his eyes came up again and locked with mine. And then he touched me. My back arched up off the bed and I cried out at the contact, feeling like I was going to explode from his touch alone.

Keeping his hand there, circling his thumb against me, he groaned and leaned down to kiss my neck, grazing his lips over my skin as they went lower until I felt his breath tickle my nipple. My body arched again, following its own urges, wanting his mouth where his breath had just lingered.

"Jag," I huskily breathed out.

He flicked his tongue out and tasted the tip of my breast, and it was as if a bolt of lightning shot through me as I cried out once again. When he sucked my nipple into his mouth, I was all but done. Oh, God, he was going to completely unravel me.

"Baby? This okay?" he stopped to ask, gazing up at me.

All I could do was nod, too overwhelmed by everything he was making me feel. We'd touched each other before, mostly hands inside jeans getting each other off, but nothing like this, so this was all so much at once, making me feel so many things, leaving me literally shaking under his touch. I could feel the intensity building inside of me as his thumb stroked me, his mouth sucking and licking at me, all of it, all of *him*, leading me to a high I knew I'd never forget.

When he slid a finger inside me, that's when I came, my body having been wound as tight as it could go before it snapped. "Oh, my God! Jag!" I screamed as my toes curled and my hips bucked up off the bed several times, my core clamping down on his finger, as I completely shattered right in front of him.

Oh, my God. Orgasms ala Jagger Jensen were fabulous. Mind blowing. Soul consuming.

As I rode out my climax, I could hear him talking softly to me the entire time, though I had no idea what he was saying. I slowly floated back from where his touch had taken me opening my eyes and looking up at him. "Hi," he said with a smile, smoothing my hair out of my face.

"Hi," I whispered back, my breath hitching and a tear slipping down the side of my face, the intensity of it all consuming me, enveloping me, shredding me to pieces as I slowly came back to myself.

He leaned down and touched his lips to mine, wiping my tear away with his thumb. "Are you all right?" he asked drawing back to look down at me, his face a mixture of what I could only decipher as concern, and then awe with a lot of lust thrown in there.

I reached up and put my hand on his face then slid it behind his head, bringing him down to kiss me again. Pulling away to look up at him, I said, "I'm more than all right, Jag. That was... unbelievable." And before I could lose my nerve, I started, "Will you..." Oh, but God, I didn't think I could take his rejection at that moment as I hesitated to ask the million dollar question. I closed my eyes and cleared my throat, swallowing nervously before opening my eyes to look into his and asked, "Will you make love to me?" Which made me turn every shade of red, of course, on top of making me hold my breath waiting to hear what he'd answer back.

He watched as he smoothed his thumb over my bottom lip before looking at me. "Baby, you sure?" he asked, his navy eyes growing heated before he bent to kiss me again, softly at first before deepening it.

Was I sure? Hell yes, I was sure. I'd been waiting to be with him my whole life. Well, technically three years because I hadn't thought about sex before then, but still.

"Yes… yes, I'm sure," I moaned against his lips, my arms wrapping around him, my fingers once again digging into the corded muscles of his back.

He pulled away from me to stand and I scooted up the bed watching as he pushed his jeans and boxer briefs down his hips.

And Jesus, Mary and holy fricking hell. I gasped as I stared at his huge, thick, hard and long erection jutting up proudly toward his stomach. Did I mention it was huge? Or thick? Hard? And long? Yeah, I think I did. I knew it was big because I'd touched it before when I'd given him hand jobs, but seeing it, him, like that? Good lord. I was certain that thing was *never* going to fit inside me.

With my mouth agape, I looked up at him, pretty sure my eyes were bugging out, to find him smirking back at me.

"Uh, Jag?" I squeaked out.

He crawled onto the bed moving toward me, looking like a predator stalking its prey, the muscles in his shoulders flexing as he moved, the smirk still gracing that beautiful face of his, which made me swallow thickly. When he got to me, he ran his hands up the front of my lower legs, over my knees then slid them up to my thighs, then pushed my legs apart with his knee, making room for his hips to come between my legs and he settled down, lying on top of me.

I was on my bed with Jagger Knox Jensen between my legs.

Naked.

And we were going to make love.

Wow.

He touched his lips to mine and pulled back to look down at me, noticing I was still a little wary about him ever fitting inside of me. "El, it'll be okay. We'll make it work. Trust me." He smiled then kissed me again more passionately turning things up as he ran his hands over me, up to caress my breasts, his mouth coming down to suck on my nipple as he rolled the other one between his thumb and finger. My hands latched onto his hair, drawing him to me as I arched off the bed when he sucked harder making a deep moan tear out of me. He moved to my other breast, doing the same, which wound me up tight, and seemingly coming from nowhere, another climax shot straight through me.

I panted his name as my body locked up, my hands clutching his hair firmly, my thighs clutching his hips tightly, as white lights flashed behind my eyes and every nerve ending in my body pulsed as if on fire. Good God, this was all so intense.

When I finally caught my breath and regained my senses some, I felt his tip at my entrance and gasped.

This was it. Finally.

"Stay with me, baby. It's okay. I'll go slow," he said before burying his face in my neck, kissing me there lightly as he rocked his hips into mine, inching inside me and whispering to me to let him know if I was okay, telling me I was beautiful, that he loved me, that he'd never wanted anyone but me.

I had my arms wrapped around him tightly, and I knew my fingernails were digging into his flesh, but I couldn't seem to stop, scared as I was. He'd never hurt me, that I knew, but with each push inside that he made, my nails just dug deeper.

"Relax, El." He pulled back to look at me, propping himself up on his muscular arms.

But, God, it was such an invasion; he was so big inside of me and it felt so strange to experience it as he stretched me farther each time he pressed into me. After he'd enter a bit more, he'd pull back out only to push in what seemed to be much deeper the next time, making me tense up even more each time.

"Baby, you've got to relax. It's okay." He brushed his lips against mine. "I love you, El. I don't want to hurt you. I'll stop if you want me to."

A drip of sweat rolled down the side of his face and I knew it was taking a lot of restraint for him to take his time with me, trying to make it easier for me. "No, keep going," I said, trying to relax, focusing on him, the feel of him, his smell, spicy and manly, watching his chest and arms flexing, his abs bunching and unbunching each time his hips rolled forward then back. He slid further inside, which felt fine until he hit a barrier and stalled.

And that kind of hurt. He remained still above me waiting for me to adjust, but the fullness inside was too much as I pushed at his shoulders, squirming under him, trying to get his huge appendage out of me. But in doing that, something inside of me hit something else just right which felt really good, and I guess my body wanted more, because I arched up suddenly. And then he was all the way in. I looked down to see us connected completely then back up at him, my eyes great big.

"How do you feel? You okay?" he asked, his voice ragged as he searched my face for any signs of despair.

"I— I'm good," I whispered looking at him still wide-eyed. He kissed me softly, then he slid out of me and pushed back inside slowly, watching me, making sure I was okay. And I was good, *it* was good. Better than good. It was amazing. "Yes, that's it, Jag. God, yes, do that again," I breathed out then moaned as he pulled out then eased back inside.

He kept up that same slow, steady pace and I closed my eyes, focusing on how it felt. And it was perfect.

I'd read all the romance novels and talked to my friends, but never did I imagine it would be like this. I was so attuned to him right then, more than I'd ever been before and it was amazing. Every nuance of what he was experiencing, of what I was experiencing, what *we* were experiencing, was laid out right there between us, and there was no hiding anything.

"Not gonna last, El. Been a long time. Sorry…" he said in a gravelly voice. "Wanna feel you come around me, though…" He leaned down and kissed me deep and wet, then slid a hand between us to work on me again, setting my body on fire, making my breath come out in gasps as I felt the buildup starting again from where his fingers caressed me, the waves of heat radiating throughout every part of my being. The push and pull of his hips was getting me hotter, the slow pump taking me even higher. "That's it, baby, come for me." God, he knew my body so well, the subtleties that he could sense when I was about to hit my peak.

Suddenly, it was too much; it felt as if he was consuming me, devouring me, possessing every last inch of me… and I loved it. I cried out his name as my climax slammed through me, my body arching off the bed, my core clamping onto him, as I lost myself around him.

When I floated back into myself, I opened my eyes to see him gazing down at me, the look in his eyes one of reverence but laced with concern.

"Was that okay?"

I reached a hand up to cup his face. "So good," I whispered on a breathy sigh, looking into his soulful eyes. God, all my firsts with him had been perfect.

"So good," he echoed, touching his lips to mine before he started moving inside me again, this time harder, stronger, more urgently as he sought his own climax.

I was in awe watching him as he gazed down at me, driving inside me, his shoulders bunching up, neck muscles tightening as he got closer to his finish. His thrusts then got shallower, tighter, as he pumped faster, harder, deeper before his body went rigid, his eyes squeezing closed as I saw the corded muscles in his neck stick out as he slammed inside deep before he threw his head back and with a curse came hard inside me. His body shuddered with his release before he collapsed on top of me, his breaths coming rapidly as he buried his face in my neck.

Oh. My. God. Sexiest thing I'd ever seen. I wrapped my arms and legs around him and kissed the side of his head, his hair damp with sweat, loving how he felt on top of me, around me, inside me.

This was another memory I knew I'd keep with me forever, one that I'd hold deep in my soul until my last breath.

He pulled back and looked down at me, eyes twinkling, crooked grin in place. "That was... God... that was good, El." He dipped down and kissed the side of my mouth, then moved his lips over my jaw and down to my neck.

I yawned. "It was," I said, not being able to keep my eyes opened anymore.

I heard him chuckle in the space between my neck and shoulder, and then I was out.

I woke up to the sound of laughter coming from the living room. Turning over, I saw that Jag was gone. My heart jumped when I thought that he might've left. Then my heart fell when I wondered if I'd dreamed his being there. But as I got out of my bed and turned to throw the covers back up, I blushed when I saw the evidence on my sheets that he'd actually been there, that he'd taken my virginity. I pulled on a sweatshirt, no bra, and panties and shorts then stripped the bed, throwing the sheets on the floor in a pile, getting new ones out of my closet, and making the bed back up. Gathering up the sheets off the floor, I left my room and went to the laundry room, throwing them inside the washing machine and starting it.

Walking into the living room, I saw Rebecca and Ross sitting on the couch talking to Jag who was in the recliner, looking handsome as ever. When he saw me, his hotness level went up twenty bajillion levels because the look on his face was so adoring, it made my stomach go all melty inside.

I smiled shyly at him as I walked over to where he sat, falling into his lap when he grabbed me around the waist and pulled me down.

"Hey," he said with a smile before kissing me softly.

"Hey," I said back then cupped his face with both my hands and leaned in to kiss him again, this time much more deeply, with tongue and everything, moaning into his mouth until I heard someone clear their throat. Crap! I'd forgotten Rebecca and Ross were in the room. I pulled back and looked at Jag, my face scrunched up in embarrassment before saying, without turning to look at Rebecca and Ross, "Hey, guys. Sorry. Forgot you were here."

Jag chuckled at that, spreading his hand at the back of my head and pulling me to him so he could touch his lips to mine again. "You're just too damned cute, baby," he said against my lips.

I blushed before turning to face my roomie and her boyfriend and waved like an idiot. "Hey."

"Hey," Rebecca said with a snort. "Nice of you to get out of bed, sleepyhead."

"What time is it?" I asked her.

"Five."

"What?" Jeez, Rocket Fuel sure was a freaking time sap. "How long have you been here?" I turned and asked Jag with a frown finally getting to the questions that'd been swirling in my head ever since I'd turned over to discover him in bed with me.

"I got here around eleven this morning," he said into my hair as he kissed the side of my head.

"Speaking of, *how* did you get here?"

"I drove," he told me with a shrug.

"Drove."

"Yes, drove."

"You drove thirteen hours to come see me?"

He sighed and looked over at Ross then rubbed a hand over the back of his neck as if embarrassed. "Yeah."

"So you drove thirteen hours… just to come see me…"

He let out a breath. "Baby, when I got those pictures of you and that guy, I lost it. I couldn't stand that he was touching you when I haven't been able to in almost three months. I couldn't take it any longer. Got in my car and left."

"But you have practice…"

"Yeah. I called Coach and told him I had a family emergency." His blue eyes pierced mine.

"You did that because you were jealous?"

He nodded slowly at me. "That and I needed to see you."

Wow.

Then a thought hit me. A not so good thought. A thought that kind of pissed me off. "Did you think I was going to cheat on you?"

He cupped my face with his hand, smoothing his thumb back and forth over my lips. "No, babe. I told you I don't worry about *you* doing anything. It's all those bastards out there hitting on you that pisses me off."

Hm. Well, at least he trusted *me*. And he'd driven all night just to be here. Wait. He'd driven all night! "Oh, God, you must be so tired!"

"Not the first time I've pulled an all-nighter, El." He chuckled. He'd moved his hand from my face to rest on my thigh where his thumb continued moving back and forth.

"We picked up your car and brought it back," Rebecca said then.

I'd forgotten all about it. Seriously, Rocket Fuel had turned me into a flaming idiot, making me forget things, lose time, and just generally be slow to think at all. Never indulging in the toxic stuff again. "Thanks, Bec," I turned and looked at her with a grateful smile.

She comically raised her eyebrows all, *Well?* wanting the down low on what'd happened between Jag and me. Her actions were so obvious that my face flushed as I looked back at her, my eyes bugging out trying to get her to stop, knowing Jag was watching our interchange.

"Dude, I need you to look at my Bronco. I think it's getting ready to throw a rod," Ross said to Jag, sparing me even more embarrassment, thank God. Ross was a classic car lover like Jag and had driven his '72 Bronco since before he and Rebecca had started dating.

"You mind, babe?" Jag asked, smirking at me, absolutely knowing that I'd be giving Rebecca all the details of our tryst once he and Ross went outside.

"Not at all," I answered him, narrowing my eyes at his smirk. Well, then, I'd just give him something more to smirk about. I leaned in and whispered in his ear, "Meet me in the shower later." Then I hopped off his lap with a smirk of my own, walked over, grabbed Rebecca's hand to pull her up off the couch and with a wicked smile over my shoulder at Jag, sashayed back to my room tugging my roommate along with me.

Chapter 12

I was two months away from turning twenty when all was right with my world.

Jag had stayed Saturday night too and left early Sunday morning so he could get back to his apartment and, in his exact words, "Get some rest from the nymphomaniac I've created." I noticed he wore a humongous smile when he said that.

What can I say? As much as I liked kissing him, he should've known that once we'd had sex, the dam would be broken and I'd only want more. I didn't hear him complaining any, though.

I'd told Rebecca everything, which had made her dance around my bedroom like a damned lunatic, making me burst out laughing. But I couldn't help feeling giddy in the fact that Jag and I were now officially a couple. After we'd talked, Rebecca told me that she and Ross would stay at his place that night so Jag and I could have more time alone. I so loved her. She was such a good friend.

After they'd looked at and worked on Ross's car, the guys had come in and had a beer before Rebecca and I came into the living room and she told Ross their plans for the night. Ross had raised an eyebrow, then with a grin punched Jag in the arm, winked at me, went to Rebecca's room to gather up some stuff, came out, kissed the top of my head, gave Jag one of those man hugs, grinned once more, told Jag he'd be talking to him soon, told us both goodbye then grabbed Rebecca's hand and they left. Well, wow. I so loved him too.

Jag then turned to me from where he sat on a barstool, and the look on his face could've melted the clothes right off me. Whoa.

"Shower?" was all he'd said before setting his beer down, getting up and stalking toward me looking all kinds of hot, his hair messy from working on Ross's vehicle, a little smudge of grease on his face.

I gulped before squeaking out in a whisper, "Yeah?"

As he prowled toward me like some jungle cat, instinct, I guess it was, made me back away from him until I hit the wall. And still he kept coming toward me, that damned crooked grin on his face making every part of me go hot for him. When he made it to me, he pressed his body into mine, looking down at me, his eyes heated.

"*Yeah?* My girl first teases me with a shower and now she's questioning it?" He pressed his hips against my stomach so I could feel that he was serious about this shower business.

Holy shit. I guess he was finished with wearing kid gloves when it came to me. He'd been all in protective mode with me before, but now the playing field was leveled. We were going by a new set of rules, and I couldn't have been more thrilled as I felt a shiver go through me.

"Not questioning it," I breathed out, looking up at him.

His mouth twitched. "No?" he asked, eyebrow raised, looking sexier than ever.

"No," I whispered.

He leaned down and brushed his lips over mine, his hands running down my back then down farther to cup my butt as he jerked me roughly into him. He pulled back and looked down at me, his eyes smoldering. Gah! I'd seen him worked up before, but this was new. This wasn't just about hands sneaking inside jeans or under a bra. This was leading to serious stuff now, and it was hot. His mouth took mine again, his tongue wrapping around mine, making a sound come from deep inside my throat that I couldn't even describe. Damn. One of his hands then snaked up and he wrapped his fingers into my hair, tugging my head back as his lips attacked my neck. Wow and double damn.

My hands went to the waistband of his jeans and I pulled almost frantically at his t-shirt to get it free, jerking it up, untucking it, wanting it off him. He grabbed it from behind his neck, pulling it over his head and tossing it to the floor then pulled my sweatshirt up and off me, his hands immediately cupping my bare breasts. I smoothed my hands over his sculpted chest then down to his fly as I tugged the buttons open, reaching my hand inside to stroke him. I swear he growled at that, which only served to turn me on even more than I already was.

"Shower… now…" he ground out as he pulled me up and I wrapped my legs around his waist as he carried me into the bathroom, his mouth landing hard on mine again.

He set me down and reached in to turn on the water, then turned to tug my shorts and panties down my legs before unlacing his boots and ridding himself of his jeans and boxer briefs. I still couldn't get enough of seeing him fully naked. He was built like a Greek god, so muscular and beautiful as if he'd been sculpted by one of the masters themselves. When he caught me staring at him, particularly down at his huge erection, he grinned then pulled me inside the shower with him, bending to kiss me before grabbing the bottle of shampoo. He placed me under the water to wet my hair then turned me to where my back was against his front as he proceeded to wash my hair, running his long fingers through it, which felt wonderful. After finishing my hair, he poured body wash into his hands then ran them all over my body, making me shiver.

He rinsed me off then keeping my back to his front, he wrapped his arms around me, one going across my chest where he cupped my breast in his hand, rolling my nipple between his thumb and finger, the other hand going between my legs, his fingers finding the mark immediately. I slammed my head back against his chest, my neck arching, as his fingers circled over me, his mouth coming down to kiss, nip and lick its way up my shoulder to my neck before stopping at my ear where he whispered very naughty things to me. He then slid a finger inside me while his thumb continued making swirls. All of this combined made me come so hard I was lucky he had his arm wrapped around me or I'd have collapsed on the shower floor.

When I was sure my legs were no longer rubbery and could hold me up, I turned to face him and after kissing him long and hard, I did the same for him, first washing the smudge of grease off his face then lathered up his hair. After that, I explored every stunning part of him with my hands as I spread the body wash over his broad shoulders and down his biceps, reaching around to glide them over his back and his tight butt then around to his hard chest and over his rippled abs. His body was magnificent. I rinsed the suds off his body then I did something I'd wanted to do to him for a long time. Running my hands slowly down his chest and abs, I knelt in front of him and licked the tip of his length, looking up at him and smiling when I saw the surprised look on his face. I languorously licked the underside of his shaft before taking him fully into my mouth, which made him throw his head back as he let out an, "Oh, fuck."

Moving my mouth up and down his hard length, I cupped him with my hand, squeezing gently as I gauged his reaction to my every move, wanting him to feel as good as he'd made me feel earlier.

"Jesus, El, you've got to stop, baby," he said through gritted teeth before he bent to pull me up then smashed his mouth to mine. He turned us to where the shower was at his back and pressed me against the wall continuing to kiss me before he said against my lips, "You too sore for any more, babe?" He pulled back to look at me with his deep navy eyes that I knew meant he was way turned on.

"No," I gasped out. Yeah, I was a little sore, but I wasn't going to stop this for anything. I grabbed him by the hair at the back of his neck and pulled him to me for another wet kiss.

"Wanted you for so fucking long," he ground out then grabbed my leg and hitched it over his hip, positioning himself at my entrance before driving up inside me so smoothly it made me cry out. "Feels so goddamned good," he murmured into my neck before he pulled his hips back almost leaving me empty then rolled them forward and filling me completely.

"Jag," I hissed, already feeling the burn inside as I grasped his shoulders while he kept surging back and forward, filling me over and over again.

"Let it go, El. Love how you feel around me when you come."

He dipped his head and took my nipple in his mouth, sucking hard, which made all kinds of things happen to my body as another long moan escaped me. He moved to my other breast, doing the same and I couldn't take it any more as I felt my core clench around him, then the buildup burst inside me, and I screamed out as my climax overtook me.

"That's it, give it to me," Jag drawled as he continued pumping inside me, one hand clasped around my thigh on his hip, the other at the curve of my butt anchoring me as he drove inside.

God. How could we not have been doing this all those years? I was gonna have a word with him later about withholding this from me, I thought as I kissed his shoulder, loving how he felt in my arms. I could tell he was getting closer as his thrusts shortened and his grips on my ass and thigh got tighter.

"Gonna come, babe," his husky voice breathed against my ear, as he plunged inside me harder, faster.

I pulled back to watch him because it'd been spectacular before, and I damn sure wasn't disappointed this time either. He thrust up inside me deep, burying himself to the root as he seemed to stop breathing, the veins in his neck popping out, his head snapping back as he came with a loud groan. Wow. So damned sexy.

He then rested his cheek against the top of my head, hugging me tight. We stood like that for several seconds before he kissed the top of my head and letting go of my leg, slid out of me slowly. He pressed his lips to mine softly then turned me so the water sprayed on me so I could rinse off then did the same for himself.

After we'd dressed, we ordered Chinese because we were both starving then after eating, we hit the bed. It was only eight in the evening, but I knew Jag had to be tired from driving all night.

"Love you, El," he said sleepily as he ran his hand through my hair.

"Love you too, Jag," I whispered back, my fingers running circles over his chest as I lay with my head there listening to the strong beat of his heart. When his breathing evened out, I knew he was asleep which left me to lie there thinking, a gazillion thoughts running through my mind. How was I going to survive after he left? I mean, we'd had sex now. And I really loved having sex. And I wanted to have more sex.

Dang. Had I become a total nymphomaniac or what?

To clarify, I meant I wanted to have more sex with *Jag*. Wasn't like I was gonna go all Slutlapalooza and sleep with anyone else. I'd meant it when I'd once told him that I wanted him to be my first and my only.

I also found myself going over our wedding plans as I lay there. Hey, it's not like every girl doesn't go there at least once with the guy she loves, right? And Rebecca and I had had our weddings all planned out since we were in sixth grade anyway, so it wasn't like this was a stretch.

I pictured my colors of navy and pale yellow, my bouquet of white calla lilies with pale yellow baby roses, and my dress like Cinderella's wedding dress but with a sweetheart neckline and huge skirt (hm, guess my prom dress hadn't been too far off the mark). Rebecca, of course, would be my maid of honor wearing her short, navy, chiffon, strapless dress with flirty, full skirt (see? ALL planned out), and Jag would look smoking hot wearing a navy tux with a pale yellow vest and tie as he waited for me to walk down the aisle to him.

Now that I was older, I'd probably change the reception to something more normal other than the carnival theme I'd loved when I was twelve when I'd decided we'd have at least twenty of those bouncy, Moon Jump things. Or would I? I snickered at that which made Jag turn in his sleep and kiss the side of my head before he turned over. So sweet.

With a smile on my face, I finally drifted off to visions of Jag and me riding off in a pumpkin-shaped carriage.

I was pressed against my wall (thank *God* Mom hadn't let me bring my iron bed frame) at the head of my bed, my legs wrapped around Jag's waist, and he was on his knees, driving up into me hard and deep.

I'd awakened from the nicest dream of him having his hands all over me only to realize that's what was really happening. And now here we were. I gasped his name as I felt myself go over the edge, which made him speed up his movements then he joined me.

He fell back on the bed, pulling me with him to where I sprawled on top of him, both of us breathing heavily.

"You're trying to kill me," he said on an exhale as he ran a hand down to cup my bottom.

Well, that wasn't very nice… even though I *had* woken him around ten the night before and again just after midnight to have another couple goes at him, and now it was just before six and we'd just had sex again.

"Hey, you took the lead on this one," I reminded him, pulling my head up to look down at him.

He cracked both eyes open just a little and looked at me, his mouth twitching at the sides as he shook his head. "Nympho."

I feigned shock. "Me?"

"Yeah, you," he said with a chuckle then put a hand on my face as he looked up at me with what seemed to be pure adoration. God, he could look at me like that every day and I wouldn't complain one bit.

"Keep looking at me like that and I'll make you go again," I threatened with a snort.

"Oh, you'll *make* me, huh?" he said, eyebrow arched as he moved his hand from my face slowly down my back to join his other hand at my butt and squeezed with both hands.

I dipped my head to lick his throat, running my tongue up the side of his neck and whispered in his ear, "I'll make you my sex slave." I nipped his ear lobe with my teeth.

"Nympho," he murmured as he turned us to where he was on top and when he did, I felt that he was just about ready for another go.

"Sex slave," I repeated on a moan as he leaned down and bit my neck, one of his hands coming between us, moving down so his fingers could work their magic on me.

Let's just say we both lived up to our nicknames... and then some.

"I wish you could stay," I said with a sniffle.

"I know, baby. I do too. But I've got to get back. I'll call you every hour, okay?"

It was nine Sunday morning and Jag was going back to school. I hated that stupid school and didn't care if he knew it. Screw being diplomatic and sweet and supportive. I'd already done that. Now I wanted my boyfriend with me.

When he grabbed his duffle bag from my room and set it by the front door, I couldn't help myself as I started crying harder.

"Babe, it's gonna be okay," he said, holding me close and kissing the top of my head.

"I'm so tired of you being away," I said through my tears.

"I am too. But one of these days this'll be over and we'll be together."

"When?" I asked, pulling back to look up at him, the tears running down my face. "You'll be going pro and who knows where you'll end up." I sucked in a breath. My arms were flailing now when I spoke. And everyone knows it's not a good thing when a girl's arms are flailing as she speaks.

"We'll make it work, El."

"How? You're there, I'm here. I have at least five more years of school left, so it's not like I can go with you. And now we've had sex and it was really, really, *really* good, and now I'm gonna miss you even more." Flail, flail, flail, flail.

His lips tipped up a bit and he grabbed me by the shoulders to stop all the damned flailing going on. "Babe, it's gonna be okay. I promise." He leaned down and touched my lips with his.

"I don't know if I can do this anymore," I spouted unthinkingly.

Let's just say that in the future, I needed to be sure to choose my words more wisely when I was upset.

His body went rigid and I knew I'd said the wrong thing.

"What's that supposed to mean?" he bit out, his fingers on my shoulders getting tighter.

"I-it doesn't mean anything," I said quietly, looking down as I chewed on the inside of my cheek.

"It means a fuckova lot of something, El." I looked up at him when he shook my shoulders. His eyes were narrowed. And they were navy. Shit. He was really mad. "You're not having doubts about us, are you?"

"No, Jag, I'm not having doubts. Forget I even said that because I didn't mean it." I sighed.

He sighed too and let go of my arms then ran his hands over his face and up through his hair.

God, I was ruining this. All of it. He'd driven thirteen hours to see me (even though it was most likely out of jealousy), we'd had incredible sex numerous times (and thank you, jealousy), I knew he was tired yet he'd given himself to me over and over, and now he had to drive as many hours back. God, I was nothing but a whiny jerk.

I took his hands in mine, bringing them to my mouth to kiss his knuckles, looking up at him. "I'm sorry, Jag… I love you. We'll make it work. We have for three years. What's a few more?" I looked up at him, hopeful.

I watched as his jaw clenched and unclenched, his eyes on a spot on the wall behind me.

He shook his hands from mine and ran one over his face again. "This is tough for me too, El. You think I'm down there just having a good time and playing ball. You don't think I wanna put my fist through the fucking wall when I see my friends with their girls, knowing I can't be with you?"

Oh. I hadn't thought of it like that before.

"Oh."

"Yeah." He crossed his arms over his chest. Uh oh. Standard *I'm still pissed at you* pose.

Looking into his brilliant blue eyes (that were currently sparking lightning flashes at me right then, eep!), I ran my hands over his muscular biceps then up over his shoulders and locked my fingers at the back of his neck, pulling him down to brush my lips over his. "I'm sorry. Baby, please don't be mad."

"Just can't say shit like that, El." He dropped his hands to my hips and put his forehead to mine.

I bit my bottom lip. "Sorry," I said looking up guiltily into his eyes.

"Stop," he kissed me, "apologizing," he kissed me again, "now."

"Okay. Sorry."

He pulled back, his lip curling up on one side. "El."

Realizing what I'd done, I huffed out a laugh. "Sorry, sorry!" Crap!

He shook his head and slid an arm around my waist drawing me to him. "You're a kook." Then he leaned down and kissed me, and, lord, it was so hot and wet, his tongue teasing mine, it made my knees buckle. He caught me with his other arm, wrapping it around my shoulder blades, his fingers squeezing right under my armpit, holding me as tight as I think he possibly could. The kiss continued until I went dizzy and when he pulled back and looked down at me, his eyes were an even darker navy.

Wow.

Both our chests were heaving and I heard him mumble, "Fuck," just before he put an arm under my bottom and picked me up. I wrapped my legs around his waist, my arms lacing around his neck tighter, and pressed my lips hard to his as he walked us back to my room for another round.

He left an hour later, our argument forgotten, both of us with huge smiles on our faces.

Chapter 13

I was twenty when Jag's dreams came true.

Ever been happy but miserable at the same time? Yeah. That was me—a complete walking oxymoron.

"El! I'm going to The Show!"

Jag called a week after his junior year season was over. His team hadn't made the CWS, but he'd informed me a couple months before that the draft started the first week of June and that he was projected to go pretty high in it. He was now calling from South Carolina where he and his dad had been tying up some loose ends before he came home for the summer. They'd also been waiting to see what pick he'd be then decide if he wanted to forgo his senior year.

I squealed into the phone. "Jag! That's great! I told you you'd go!"

He'd been so worried that he wouldn't get picked up—even though he'd been considered one of the top drafts in the country—and although I didn't want him to be drafted to a team that would take him even farther away from me, I was still excited for him.

"The Dodgers!"

And my face fell. Los Angeles. Wasn't that just great. I'd been holding out hope that he'd be a Cub and be right here with me. I'd even take him being a Brewer or Tiger. Or even a Toronto Blue Jay. Hell, at this point, I'd have even settled for him playing for the White Sox. But nope. He'd be about as far away as he could be. Seemed that Fate, that flaming bitch, just had it in for us. I wanted to burst into tears right then and there, but for Jag, I put on a brave front. "Awesome! That's so cool!" Tears stung the backs of my eyes and my throat had that humongous lump in it that burns and makes it hard to swallow.

"My dad hired an agent, and he says I have a signing bonus coming. Seven figures, El! I'm a millionaire!" He let out a laugh. "I'll be home in a couple days then I'm taking you out to Everest. Calling them after we hang up to make a reservation." Wow. Everest was a fancy schmancy restaurant in Chicago and I'd heard it easily cost around $300 for two to eat there. I'd be willing to bet they didn't have root beer floats.

I was glad he hadn't heard the wavering in my voice. His dreams were coming true so no way was I going to rain on his parade. He was now a real, live professional baseball player, which was pretty damned amazing. "I'm so proud of you, Jag. See? I told you it'd be easy," I said with a forced chuckle.

He laughed. "Yeah, pretty easy, considering I've thrown around ten thousand pitches in my life to get where I am."

"Think you got ten thousand more in you?" I teased.

"I hope. El, this is it. Our ticket to the big time."

Our.

Okay, now I felt like shit for being upset. He was still including me in everything like he always did. I wished my vision of the future was as positive as his was. I knew I seriously needed to douse the Eau de Bitch that was threatening to waft off me. "I'm so happy for you, Jag."

"*Us*, babe."

"Yeah."

After hanging up, I called Rebecca who was at work. "Bec," I choked out.

"El? You okay?" she asked.

"It's bad, Bec. Can you talk for a minute?"

I heard her telling our manager that she needed a break then I heard her tennis shoes squeaking on the floor as she walked outside. "Okay, what's going on?" she asked, concern lacing her voice.

I instantly burst out crying. "It's Jag," I sobbed out.

"What? Is he okay?"

"Yes, but he just went pro!" I cried.

I heard her chuckle. "God, you scared me! Uh, sorry, but I'm not seeing the bad here, El."

I sniffed. "He signed with the Dodgers."

"And that's bad why?" she asked still totally clueless.

"It's bad because they're in Los Angeles! Well, he'll have to play in Albuquerque on their minor league team first, but he's good, so he'll probably get called up after one season."

"Oh. Oh! Damn, El, I'm sorry," she consoled. She knew how hard the past three years had been on me with Jag and I being apart and now we were faced with more of the same. Yay.

"Thanks, Bec," I said with a snuffle.

"What are you gonna do?"

"What *can* I do?" I asked.

"Um, go with him?"

I paused for a beat.

"El?"

"Yeah, I just thought I heard you tell me to go with him. Must be a bad connection."

She laughed. "You heard me right. Go with him."

I'd never even given going with Jag a thought. Hm. That just might work. Unless he didn't want me with him. And I had to consider what my parents would say. "I don't know, Bec. I'd wait until his first year's over anyway because he'll be so busy," I told her. He'd be busy every year after, but the first year I figured would be more stressful.

"So when he goes to LA, go then. USC has, like, the top physical therapy school in the country. You could transfer there easily. And you'd only have two years left since you're on the fast track to graduating already."

"I don't know if it'd be a good idea," I said.

"*I* think it's a great idea. Why don't you spring it on him?"

"I'm sure he'd love a springing of that nature." I rolled my eyes. *Oh, by the way, Jag, I'm coming with you. You don't mind, do you?* Ugh.

"When's he coming home?"

"He said in a couple days. His dad's renting a trailer and they're loading all his stuff and moving him back here until he has to go to Albuquerque. He said he's taking me to Everest when he gets home."

Rebecca squealed. "Oh my God! I've wanted to go there forever! Lucky!"

"I know. I'll bring you a doggie bag shaped like Mt. Everest. You think that's what they do? I have no idea why the place is named that. But, I mean, I guess I can shape the damned thing into a peak myself. Wouldn't take a whole lot of talent."

"Yeah, they probably train some poor idiot for weeks making sure he gets the summit just right." We burst out laughing at that.

"Thanks, Bec. I needed to laugh right now."

"It'll be okay, El. Promise."

Between her and Jag always promising me that everything would be okay, I felt that things actually would be okay. It was just getting to the place that they were okay that got to be a little tedious at times.

"Thanks, Bec. I love you, you know?"

"Yeah. I know. What's not to love?" She chuckled. "And I hope you know I love you too."

She'd been my best friend forever, and I couldn't help thinking that even though I wanted things to work out with Jag, I'd still hate leaving her.

"Wow," I breathed out looking out at the Chicago skyline.

Jag and I sat at a window seat at Everest, which was located on the fortieth floor of the Chicago Stock Exchange Building, and the view was literally breathtaking.

"Nice, huh?" he said with a smirk. I knew he was very pleased to have been able to take me here now that money was really no object for him since his signing bonus had been deposited into his checking account the day before.

"Very," I agreed grinning back at him. He was looking pretty cute in all his smugness, I thought. He wore fame well, as I always knew he would.

He and his dad had just come in from South Carolina the night before and he'd called en route to let me know we'd be dining out tonight. It hadn't given me a lot of time to get someone to cover me at work or to get an outfit together, but I'd managed both and the cocktail dress I'd found was pretty kickass. It was an LBD that had a section of lace at the midriff then another that went up from the bodice to the collar. The kickass part was my whole back was bared to my waist. I topped the outfit off with thigh highs that had a back seam, black stilettos, all of which made me feel damned sexy. The "Fuck me" that Jag had mumbled when he'd first seen me let me know I'd chosen well.

Sitting there at the table, he was looking damned good himself wearing black slacks, a black button down shirt with no tie, the top two buttons undone, and a charcoal gray sports coat. His hair was longer than normal and I liked the way it looked, arranged all messily. Funny how when you haven't seen someone on a regular basis you notice things you normally wouldn't and all of it looked great on him. As I sat across the table looking at him, I realized that although he'd been a very good looking teenager, he was now a stunningly handsome man.

He quirked his mouth up on one side. "What?"

I came out of my mini daze with a start, unaware that I'd been staring at him. Ogling, really. "You're so handsome, Jag," I blurted then blushed. But my mouth wasn't finished. "You look so sexy in that shirt and coat. And, God, your five-o'clock shadow is freaking hot!" I snapped my mouth shut quickly. It wasn't that I didn't mind giving him compliments. God knew that what I said was true, but I hated that he could make me ramble on like that.

He smirked even more at that before he leaned over the table toward me, which made me lean toward him. "You're gonna think it's really hot later when I'm rubbing it against the inside of your thighs." I pulled back to look at him in surprise and saw that his eyes were navy. "I can't wait to be inside you, El."

Holy shit. The hungry look on his face literally made me gulp. My legs involuntarily came together in a clench as I wriggled in my chair, the butterflies inside me dancing around like crazy as I felt my panties dampen. "Jag," I whispered, my eyes practically bugging out as I looked around surreptitiously to make sure no one had heard him. "You can't talk like that here!" I said, still whispering and still looking around.

But my eyes were only on his when he reached over and took my hand, pulling me back toward him again. "I can say whatever I damn well please, El, and I mean it when I say I can't wait to fuck you."

If my mind were a keyboard, it'd be typing out all kinds of those symbol things because he was scrambling my brain with what he was saying. It was all I could do to keep from using my napkin as a fan. Our waiter decided to show up just then with the amuse-bouches, and Jag reluctantly let my hand go. I still felt his eyes on me as the waiter explained what each item was, and at first, I was so damned hyperaware of Jag that I couldn't even concentrate on what our server was saying, but as he continued describing it all, I became so enthralled, even asking him questions, that I moved away from my previously unsettled state. When he left the table, I looked up to see Jag still watching me, his dark eyes still boring into mine. Whoa.

"Maybe we should've skipped dinner," I whispered.

When Jag had picked me up at my apartment earlier, he'd given me a kiss to end all kisses, but I'd stupidly insisted that we stay on schedule, reminding him that he'd made the reservation at Everest several days in advance, we were already dressed and that we didn't want to be late. Besides, Rebecca and Ross had been there (she'd promised that they'd be gone for the night, though) so it wasn't like we could just jump in bed and get down to business, right?

He reached across the table and took my hand again, smoothing his thumb over the backs of my knuckles as he continued giving me *the look*. "Maybe. But I do like the anticipation."

Dear God. I was gonna spontaneously combust with all the damned heat that was running through my veins. I took a deep breath then focused on the hors d'oeuvres, offering him a taste of my lobster even though he had his own. Hey, I was flustered! But as he leaned forward, his eyes on mine, and took my fork in his mouth, his gorgeous lips so sexy as they closed around it, I was done for. "Wa—wanna leave?" I stammered.

His lips twitched as he sat back and shook his head slowly, his eyes still on mine while he chewed, the muscles in his jaws bulging with each bite. Then his Adam's apple bobbed as he swallowed. *Then* he licked his lips. He definitely had this seduction thing down, and I don't even think he was trying. I closed my gaping mouth and crossed my legs for what seemed like the fiftieth time. How could he be sitting there all cool and calm while I was a veritable horny mess?

The waiter brought the next course, the second out of seven. After this, only five more stages of foreplay to go. God, this was sweet torture. What made me feel better was when I got up to use the women's room after the third course had been delivered, Jag had nabbed me by the wrist, pulling me to him for a quick kiss and I saw that he was sporting a huge erection. I looked at him in surprise as he narrowed his eyes at me. Well, at least he had to suffer too, I thought with a chuckle as I walked away from the table.

"Oh, my God, Jag…" I breathed out.

We'd made it home from Everest and had barely made it in the door of my apartment before we'd stripped each other naked, though I'd kept my heels and stockings on at Jag's insistence. He now had me pinned against the door, one hand splayed across my stomach as he knelt in front of me. He'd thrown one of my legs over his shoulder and was now languidly dragging his tongue up the inside of my thigh, his scruff brushing against my skin just as he'd promised. My fingers were laced in his hair, and when his other hand moved up and he slipped a finger inside me, pressing it in the right place, I gasped then clutched his hair hard as my leg buckled and I teetered on my five-inch heel.

"Easy, baby," he muttered, looking up at me, his dark eyes brimming with lust. Oh my.

His lips eased their way higher as he kept watching me, and when they landed on my softest parts, he sucked me inside his hot mouth. I lost it then, scorching waves of pleasure radiating throughout my entire body, and screaming his name, I came harder than I ever had before. He didn't stop until he was sure he'd wrung as much of my climax out of me as he could and my body was near collapse. Wow. He gently took my leg off his shoulder with a kiss at my knee then stood slowly, running his tongue over my stomach, kissing and nipping here and there, stopping to suck in each nipple, making my breath catch when burning spasms rippled through me once again.

After coming to his full height, he wrapped a hand in the hair at the nape of my neck, grasping my butt with his other hand and kissed me deeply. Then it seemed as if he couldn't wait any longer and he grabbed me, turning me roughly to face the couch, bending me over the back of it. He nudged my legs apart, his foot pushing my foot to the side, then his hands came to my hips, I felt his knees bend slightly behind me and he slid his length up inside me, then thrust up so fast and going so deep I cried out his name again as my fingers clutched the sofa cushions.

"Told you…" he murmured between thrusts, "couldn't wait… to fuck you… El…" He drove up hard inside me, digging his fingers so hard into my hips I'd probably bruise, but I couldn't have cared less. Oh, I liked this side of him, wanting me so badly that he was almost blind with desire.

"Jesus," he rasped as one of his hands smoothed up my spine and into my hair where he twisted his fingers, fisting his hand in it and pulling my head back. He leaned into me, his scruff brushing against my cheek as he huskily said, "You like me fucking you, El? Like my cock inside you?" His other hand had wound its way around to my stomach and down where his fingers went between my legs, rubbing over me, which made my core spasm a little around him and I sucked in a breath as the burn inside threatened to explode throughout my body.

"Oh, my God, Jag…" I panted.

He yanked on my hair, pulling my head back again and hissed in my ear, "Answer me."

Oh. He'd asked me a question. Right. "Yes, Jag. Yes. I love you inside me. God, yes." And I did love it. *Loved* it. I never thought his being a little rough with me would turn me on, but holy shit did it ever.

Pumping up inside me, he kept both hands where they were, one with his fingers rolling over me threatening to drive me mad, the other balled in my hair turning me on like nothing else.

He pulled out then, turning me to face him, his mouth coming down hard on mine as one of his arms slipped behind me and across my lower back and the other dipped down under my bottom to lift me up. My legs wrapped around his waist, arms going around his neck, and he walked us to my bedroom, his lips never leaving mine. After sitting down on the edge of my bed, he lifted me at the hips and slid his length inside me again.

"Oh, shit," I gasped. He was so deep this way. I put the toes of my stilettos between the mattresses for leverage and grabbed his shoulders as I moved myself up and down on him.

"Fuck," he said with a groan, his voice all sexy and hoarse and gravelly as he looked down at where we were joined, his hands sliding up my thigh highs then going back to my hips as he watched me roll them to take him deeper. "Touch yourself, El," he growled. I stopped moving on him and with my eyes big, looked into his dark eyes as they glittered with lust back at me. I'd never done that before in front of him and it'd taken me a little off-guard. At my hesitation, he commanded, "Do it."

Although I loved this macho, alpha side of him that came out during sex, I stayed still, unsure of doing that in front of him. He pushed off the floor on the balls of his feet, jerking his hips up hard, impaling me deep then said in a warning tone, "El."

Oh, God. I licked my lips as I slowly moved a hand from his shoulder down, still reluctant to do what he'd ordered while he watched. He leaned in then and kissed me hard, his lips bruising mine as he took my hand in his, placing it where he wanted it, his fingers over mine, guiding them to move in circles just above where we were connected before he pulled back, looking down at our hands.

Oh, damn. This was completely hot. Feeling more confident at the satisfied smirk on his face, I took over and he moved his hand to grip my hip again, using both hands now to move me up and down on him.

"Fuck yeah," he growled.

It didn't take long until I was there, and I threw my head back as I cried out his name. He joined me not long after, holding my hips tightly to his as he plunged up inside as deep as he could go. We were both breathing heavily, our bodies misted with sweat when he leaned in and kissed my forehead, his arms wrapping firmly around me. "That was hot, El," he said between breaths. "So... fucking... hot."

"I love you," I murmured against his neck, nuzzling into him, my body completely sated.

He squeezed me in a deep hug, kissing the top of my head, and I fell asleep right there in his arms with him still inside me, knowing I was right where I belonged.

Chapter 14

I was twenty-one when Jag and I were finally going to begin our life together.

We were only able to spend a week together after our night at Everest. The baseball season was well on its way and Jag was to report almost immediately. He planned to fly to Albuquerque and stay in a hotel until he found an apartment or condo to stay in, maybe room with one of the other players.

We'd talked before he left, though, and cleared up so many things that by the time he left, I felt a kabillion times better than I had since he'd gotten drafted.

"Um, so you'll be in Albuquerque for a year?" I asked.

"That's the plan. I mean, it could be longer, but I hope I get called up before then." I'd made crab and ricotta cannelloni, his favorite, and we sat at the little dining table in my apartment.

"You will," I said with a smile, taking a drink of wine. "You're an amazing pitcher. They're crazy not to take you now."

He laughed. "Yeah, well, that's hardly protocol. I mean, it'd be cool, but most guys spend a year in the minors, so that'll be me."

"Then on to LA, huh?" I asked. Ugh. I was afraid to bring this next part up. What if he said no? I took another drink of wine, trying to get my nerve up.

"Hopefully."

"So..."

He looked up at me as he took another bite. "God, this is good, El. I love when you make this."

"Thanks. I know you do. I wanted to do something nice before you leave."

He leaned over and gave me a quick kiss. "Well, thank you."

"You're welcome."

We continued eating in silence. Well, he continued eating while I drank trying to build courage. After a few minutes, he took his last bite then looked at me until I finally met his eyes. "All right. What's going on?"

"Nothing." Crap. My deer in the headlights look at his question totally gave me away.

"Yeah, whatever. What's up?"

"Well…" I got up and started clearing dishes from the table. "I, uh, was talking to Rebecca the other day."

Jag sat back turning his chair so he could see me in the kitchen. "You want some help?"

"No, no, I'm good. Stay there and I'll bring you some cake," I replied.

I got a knife and forks out of a drawer along with plates and pulled the chocolate cake I'd made toward me on the counter. I looked over at him seeing that he was intently watching me, waiting to hear what I had to say. I turned away to cut two pieces then carried them to the table, putting his in front of him before I sat down.

"Good?" I asked after he'd taken a bite.

"Delicious," he mumbled, mouth full.

More silence filled the room except for our forks scraping on the plates as we ate. I guess he got fed up with waiting because his fork clanked down on his plate loudly making me jump in my seat.

"What the fuck's going on, El?"

Great. Now I'd pissed him off while trying to make him happy by making all of his favorite foods. The intense look on his face told me that I needed to get this discussion rolling sooner rather than later. Taking a deep breath, I began. "You're gonna be in Albuquerque for a year, right?"

"Mm hm." He'd crossed his arms at his chest as he looked at me.

"So it'd kinda be like you were in your senior year anyway, right?"

"Mm hm."

"So it's not like we're losing any time 'cause if you were at SC, it'd still be the same."

"El…" He was losing patience.

"My point is that this year wouldn't really be any different from the past two."

"Okay."

"But when you go to LA…"

I guess he could see how really nervous I was because he leaned over and grabbed me by the arm, pulling me out of my chair to sit in his lap. "What's on your mind, baby?" He tucked a piece of hair behind my ear.

I swallowed roughly. Why was this so hard to ask? Well, duh. Because if he said no, it'd hurt me big time. "Well, the University of Southern California has a really great physical therapy school. It's rated the best in the nation, actually."

Putting a finger under my chin, he turned my face toward his. "You wanting to come to Los Angeles with me, El?"

I raised my eyebrows, looking at him hopefully. "Yes?"

He chuckled then kissed the tip of my nose. "I'd love that."

Oh.

Oh! Well, that was easy.

"Really?" I squealed.

"Really," he said then kissed me for real. Then he stood and carried me to my bedroom and proceeded to show me how much he loved the idea of my coming to LA with him, and I was more than happy to reciprocate.

Jag's first year in the minors went somewhat quickly to my surprise. I think it may have been that I was so busy with school and work, so focused on moving forward in my degree, or maybe it was that I kept the idea of moving to Los Angeles to be with him in the forefront of my mind. Whatever it was, I was glad for it because I missed him terribly.

But I have to say, whoever invented texting was a frickin' genius because it got me through some pretty rough times when I really missed him and we didn't have time to call. Also, gobs of sessions of sexting with Jag helped tons because I missed having sex with him. A lot. We sent so many risqué pictures to each other that I was pretty sure after that year I could pick out Jag's penis in a police lineup any old day.

The season had been April through September and since he'd left here at the end of June, he'd only gotten to play the last three months of it. But the organization had decided he was the "real deal" because they called him up in October. He'd been so excited when he called to let me know. I was at work but proceeded to whoop and holler right there in Starbucks causing the customers to throw me dirty looks since it was fairly early in the morning when I got his call.

The next week, Jag's parents flew out to Albuquerque to help him make the move to Los Angeles and help him find a place to live. I'd wanted to go, but I was in the middle of midterm exams, so during the packing and the move, he'd kept me updated by text. I almost got kicked out of my anatomy midterm because he'd sent me a ridiculous picture of himself trying to look like some badass gang member in front of his packed car, flashing gang signs and all, his baseball cap sitting sideways on his head. I busted out laughing then had to cover it with a series of coughs when the professor gave me the evil eye. I should've known better than to check my stupid phone when it'd buzzed.

His parents had rented a car when they got to Albuquerque and planned to follow him as they drove the almost twelve hours to Los Angeles, all of them planning to stay in a hotel when they got there. He'd been staying in a small, furnished apartment during his stay in Albuquerque, so all he had to move were his clothes, toiletries and a few other smaller items, so they hadn't needed a truck.

He sent pictures all during the day, some of him driving, some of him at convenience stores filling up his car or (and this is so telling of what a *guy* he was) going to the bathroom. Not that he actually sent pictures of himself peeing. I think I would've turned my phone off if that'd been the case. No, he just sent several pictures of bathroom doors, which made me laugh and roll my eyes.

Just after midnight that night, my phone rang, waking me.

"'Lo?" I answered sleepily.

"Baby. I love how your voice sounds so husky and throaty when you've been asleep."

"Jag…" I whispered.

"I miss you."

"Miss you too. Wish I could've gone with you," I said with a yawn.

"Me too. You awake now?"

"Yeah," I said, sitting up and rubbing the sleep out of my eyes.

"Just calling to let you know we made it to the hotel in LA. We're gonna stay here a couple days until I can find a place. Then Mom and Dad will be taking off. Mom's dying to go up to Napa Valley to go on some six-hour wine tasting tour thing. Dad's thrilled, as you can imagine."

I chuckled. Mrs. Jensen was a huge wine enthusiast, but Mr. Jensen hated it and let everyone know that he was strictly a bourbon man. "I'm sure he'll have fun."

"Don't count on it. Tomorrow we're gonna hit up a realtor and look around at some places. I'll send pictures."

"As long as they're not of the bathroom, I'm good," I said, laughing.

"Aw, babe, you take all the fun out of it." He laughed with me.

I giggled at his silliness. "God, I miss you so much."

"Same. But I'll find us a place and you'll be out here end of December. Then it'll all be good. How about that?"

"Sounds perfect. I can't wait."

"Me either. Well, I'm beat. Gotta get some sleep. That drive is a killer. Love you. I'll call you tomorrow."

"Love you too."

We hung up and when I woke up the next morning, I was all smiles from the awesome dream I'd had of Jag and me living together in LA.

Jag came home over Thanksgiving and we
spent the entire week together. It was great having uninterrupted time to just be with each other. He'd found a gorgeous condo (he'd sent lots of pics) to rent in Santa Monica that was practically on the beach, and I couldn't wait to go out and see it.

"El, it's so cool. I bought a surfboard and one of the guys on the team said he'd teach me how to surf."

We sat on the sofa at my apartment talking. I'd made dinner and now we were just hanging out.

"You're gonna turn into a beach bum, I can already tell."

He grinned at that. "Maybe. If it means I get to see you in a bikini all the time, then hell yeah, that's what I'll become."

How he could still make me blush amazed me, but my face turned a deep red, which made him laugh as he leaned in to touch his lips to mine.

"So what are the other tenants around you like?"

He shrugged. "Just your usual California people, I guess. There's an old man, probably in his seventies across the hall from me. Mr. Ashton. I've helped him get his groceries in a couple times. I've also met the couple that lives across and down the hall from me, the Lenoxes. They're in their fifties and really nice, but they pretty much keep to themselves."

"Nice and quiet, huh?"

"Yeah. But I love sitting out on the patio at night. If there's a concert going on at the Pier, I can hear it. And the smell of the ocean is awesome. It just makes you feel so, I don't know, alive or something."

"It sounds wonderful. I can't wait to see it."

"I can't wait for you to be there with me either. I'll feel a lot better once you're there."

I frowned. "What do you mean?"

He shrugged again then squeezed my thigh. "Nothing. I just miss you."

I'd had my bags packed two weeks before Christmas, right after my last semester final, so excited to go to LA with Jag. I'd talked to my parents about transferring and going to live with him before the semester had even begun, and to my complete and utter shock, they'd supported the idea from the start. I guess since Jag and I'd been a couple for going on five years, not including all the years we'd been together when we were little, they finally accepted that we were *together-together* and were willing to let me go. Mom had cried, saying that her little girl was now a woman (yeesh), and Dad had just looked at me as if he knew every sordid sexual thing Jag and I had done together (double yeesh).

Jag's parents were way onboard with the idea, wanting someone, in the words of Mrs. Jensen, to "keep Jag grounded in case he got the 'big head' from being a professional athlete." Well, that and she said at least he'd have someone to make sure that he kept his toilet cleaned. Seriously, what was with his family and bathrooms?

I'd been accepted into USC's Physical Therapy Program since several of my professors had contacted the school on my behalf, letting them know that I was a good candidate. I'd busted my ass over the past two years to get early acceptance into

Northwestern's Physical Therapy Program, and USC had taken all my credits, thank God, so things would pretty much be set if my interview went well.

Jag had come home for Christmas and things couldn't have been any more perfect. I'd aced my semester finals, he'd been doing great in his workouts with his trainer, and we'd be driving out two days after the holiday and would be spending New Year's in LA. To say I was stoked was putting it mildly.

Christmas day, all my brothers came home for lunch, Mike and Jake with their wives and Robbie with his girlfriend. They all lived and worked in the Chicago area, so it wasn't like we hadn't seen each other in years, but it was great that we could all get together. Jag came over too, and my brothers were all excited for him to be playing in the pros telling him they thought it was awesome. We ate then opened presents, and when we'd finished digging into our gifts like we were still kids, I got a little teary-eyed when Mom announced through her own tears to everyone that I'd be leaving for California in two days.

"It's not like I'll be gone forever," I whispered, trying not to choke up. Jag sat beside me on the couch and threw his arm around my shoulders, pulling me into his side, and kissed the side of my head.

"Always knew you'd make it big," Jake said as he got up to get another mug of eggnog, punching Jag in the arm playfully as he walked by.

"Thanks, man," Jag said with a grin.

"Same here," Mike added from where he sat in the loveseat with his wife. "But, damn, the least you could've done is held out for the Cubs or another more reputable team."

Jag barked out a laugh at that. "Hey, gotta go where the money is, I guess," he replied.

"We'll be watching you," Robbie threw in from where he and his girlfriend sat on the floor in front of the fireplace. He and I were the closest, I guess because we were closest in age, and that had always made him the most protective of me. "Better keep El happy." I thought he'd been teasing, but the look on his face said differently.

"Robbie," I scolded when I felt Jag tense a little beside me.

"I'll do my best," Jag promised, leaning down to kiss the side of my head again.

My parents and I had Christmas dinner at Jag's parents' house and we were also joined by his sister and her husband. The evening was great and I was glad we'd gotten to spend the day with all our relatives.

When we were back at my apartment, Jag and I exchanged gifts. I'd gotten him some sex wax for his surfboard, which made him laugh, and I'd framed the sports page from the local paper that had announced that he'd been drafted. I was a poor college student and couldn't afford a whole lot, but he loved it just the same.

He'd gotten me a Beauty and the Beast figurine that made my heart melt. His other gift was a Tiffany's necklace with a heart locket that had inscribed on the back "Forever and a day." I'd burst out in tears after I'd opened it to see a picture of us when we were little, holding hands and laughing as we looked at each other, and one of us from the past Thanksgiving when we'd been outside watching some of the neighbor kids playing football and we were practically in the same pose. His mom had taken care of getting the pictures put in the locket, but overall I had to say he'd done excellent in the gift department.

We hung out with Rebecca and Ross all the next day. She was keeping the apartment, and I'd planned on having my dad come and move my stuff out, but she'd thrown a fit, begging me to leave it so that in case I ever came back to visit, I could sleep in my room again. I didn't want to argue with her, and Mom and Dad would've had to sell it all anyway, so I just left it where it was. That evening when the guys were in the living room playing some video game Rebecca had gotten Ross for Christmas, she and I were in my bedroom sitting on my bed and having a good cry.

"Remember, El, I'm keeping the apartment, so if things don't work out…"

I blew air out of my mouth in a "Pffttt" kind of way. "Bec, Jag and I were meant to be. They say long-distance relationships don't work, but by God, we've lasted this long, so I know nothing's gonna happen. Besides, we're getting married someday anyway, so you can just keep the stuff and if you ever want a roommate, she'll be all set up. Or I'll use it whenever I'm back in town to visit."

"I still can't believe you're going," she said with a sniffle.

"I know. Is it okay to tell you I'm scared shitless? I've never been out of Illinois except for vacations and ballgames. What if I hate it? What if he's never home? What if the baseball wives don't like me? Am I gonna be okay?" I asked, my voice going up an octave as more questions I hadn't even thought of before flooded my mind. I had to admit, this was freaking scary.

She laughed through her tears. "You'll be fine, babe. Everyone will love you. And he's bound to be gone for games, of course, but you'll be okay. Think of all that study time you'll have." Then she waggled her eyebrows. "Think of how it'll be when he gets back home."

I blushed. "Yeah."

"I'll miss you so damned much, El. We've been best friends since third grade." She started crying harder which made me cry harder. "What am I gonna do without my bestie?"

I hugged her tight, and cried along with her. "I'm just a phone call away, Bec."

I didn't know then that *I'd* be the one calling on my bestie in a year to help me get out of 'the worst mess of my life.

Jag and I left for LA the next day, planning to make stops for the night in Omaha, Denver, and lastly, Las Vegas before reaching our final destination, Santa Monica. Jag had flown home for Christmas, so we were driving my Jetta, which was cram-packed with my clothes and other things, such as books for classes and random stuff I thought I might need. Jag had told me we'd get whatever else I needed when we arrived, so I was okay with what I'd packed, only having a minor freak out as I triple checked to make sure I had everything.

Rebecca and I had a tearful goodbye, I hugged Ross, Jag hugged Rebecca, Jag and Ross did the guy hug thing and we left, heading to each of our parents' houses, stopping at Jag's first. Mrs. Jensen, bless her heart, gave us one of those coffee carafes that had a pump, and much to my delight she'd filled it with white chocolate mocha from Starbucks. She'd also packed two travel mugs in a little basket along with, be still my freaking heart, pumpkin cream cheese muffins. She'd also put a can of whipped cream in the basket so we could put it on our drinks. Oh, how I loved her for all of it.

We left their house and drove down to the end of the block to my house where I had another tearful goodbye with my parents. Dad made Jag promise to have me call home every hour before he'd even let us out the door to leave. Jag told him he was on it. Hugs were given all around then we got in the car. As we took off, I hooked up my iPod, turning on some Soundgarden, pumped mocha into a mug for Jag, and before handing it to him, squirted some whipped cream on top of it, which got me a dirty response from him about all the things we could do with the whipped cream later, which made me giggle, I fixed my own mug, then got out a muffin for each of us.

I was giddy but also a little sad when we got on the interstate, heading out of Chicago. Giddy to start a new life with Jag; sad to leave my family and friends behind. But when Jag grabbed my hand and squeezed while giving me a reassuring smile, I knew everything was going to be just fine.

"Favorite slasher movie."

"Easy. *I Still Know What You Did Last Summer.*" Jag looked at me smugly.

We'd been on the road for four hours and were really getting to know a different side of each other through the sophisticated game we were playing. That was sarcasm, of course. The Question Game wasn't really that complicated. Jag was driving and we were swapping inquiries back and forth, but we really were finding out new things about each other.

"You're kidding, right?" I cut my eyes suspiciously at him. That movie was crap.

"Babe." He said that as if it were an explanation.

I now looked at him, eyebrows raised. He looked back at me as if I were supposed to know what he meant. "What?" I finally questioned.

"I was thirteen. Snuck into the theater with Tyler Callihan. Jennifer Love Hewitt in a tank top? One of my top five favorite movies of all time."

I made a face. "So, basically, you're telling me she was good jack-off material."

He snorted. "Basically, yeah."

"Guys." I shook my head.

"I was thirteen, El. Her tits were spectacular in that movie." I smacked his arm and he grabbed my wrist pulling me into him. Keeping an eye on the road but leaning down to me, he said, "That is until I got a glimpse of yours." He kissed me quickly then let me go.

"Crude."

He puffed his chest out with pride. "That's me."

I shook my head again and laughed. "Your turn."

"Favorite position?"

Almost every one of his questions had been sexual, so instead of fighting it like I had the others, I just went with it. Although I still blushed like mad. "I really liked that one time…"

He glanced at me in surprise that I was actually going to answer him. Then he looked at me again, not so patiently waiting to hear my answer. I bit my lip, feeling stupid that I was still shy about talking about sex with him.

"That one time… Got me curious, El."

Damn it. Okay, I could do this. "The time I woke up and you were, uh, spooning me…" He looked over at me, brows drawn down as if he didn't remember. Jerk. He was going to make me say it. Ugh. "We'd been asleep, and I woke up… and you had your hand, um, down there…"

"Down where, El?" And there he was: Super Alpha Male Jag, getting all bossy whenever it came to sex, forcing me to say the words out loud.

"Down *there*."

"El…"

"And you were rolling your fingers over my…"

"Over your clit?" He looked over at me with a sexy grin.

Bastard.

"Yes," I said quietly. I *had* to get over being this shy when it came to talking about sex.

"Then what?"

I had to admit. This *was* kind of hot. I shifted in my seat feeling myself getting a little turned on. "Then you… you entered me… from behind…"

"Liked that, didn't you?" His voice was deeper now, and I knew he was getting turned on too.

I had liked it. A lot. With my face burning, I looked directly at him. "Yes. I did. I loved it, actually." Then I uncharacteristically reached over and rubbed my hand on his crotch. He was halfway erect. Wow.

He groaned. "God, El, you're getting me hard. We've still got over an hour to Omaha. You don't stop, I'm gonna pull over and have you right here."

I didn't stop, so we wound up in Des Moines and got a hotel for the night. Ha. Maybe I was bad at the sex talk, but I made up for it in other areas.

We'd stopped in Denver the next evening and left the next morning for Las Vegas. I was having a great time on the trip and I think Jag was too. I'd been a little afraid that spending so much time together might make us a little irritated with each other since it wasn't the norm, but we were having a blast, discussing everything from personal stuff to the landscape to the weather. We'd both thought it was cool how the snow had just suddenly disappeared the farther west we went. Denver had been covered in it, and then it was just… gone.

We arrived in Vegas around eleven that night, and after checking into the Bellagio (*the Bellagio!)* we walked The Strip taking in all the sights, stopping in several other hotels to play the slots and Jag tried his hand at Blackjack and Roulette a couple times. We stayed out a little later than we'd expected to, but we only had about a four and a half our drive the next day, so it wasn't a big deal. When we were finished seeing the sights, we went up to our room and he told me that the next time we went to Vegas, he'd be "known" and would arrange for us to have a villa. The room we had was beyond gorgeous so I could only imagine what a villa would look like.

We left around one the next afternoon and arrived at Jag's condo at six that evening, and boy, was I just dazzled as hell. His place was spectacular! It *so* hadn't translated at all in the pictures he'd sent. I don't know how he'd kept from telling me more about it than he had because it was all kinds of fabulous. I ran to the French doors off the kitchen right off the bat, looking out to see the beach and squealing at how freaking cool that was. He led me out onto the patio and I fell absolutely in love with his place. I could hear the sounds from the Pier and I looked at him with a huge grin on my face.

"We'll go down there in a bit if you want."

Oh, I wanted! I went up on my tiptoes, wrapping my arms around his neck and kissed the fool out of him. This was going to be good. I knew it to my bones that my coming there to be with him was where I was supposed to be.

Chapter 15

I was almost twenty-two when I discovered that Jag was likely the most wanted man on the planet.

January in Santa Monica was awesome.

Jag wasn't very busy at all. Besides meeting with his trainer every day or having meetings with the team's manager or other staff, I had him to myself most of the time, which was cool. He'd shown me around the city and taken me on the I-10 over to the university, which had been a piece of cake. It was a straight shot to get there so I wasn't worried about finding it. We'd driven around campus so I could see where my classes would be and it was all I could do to keep from bouncing up and down in my seat I was so ready to start.

Besides walking to the Santa Monica Pier, we took in various other sites including, of course, Hollywood Boulevard where we saw the handprints of the stars outside of Mann's Chinese Theater, we walked the Walk of Fame, and went on one of those cheesy tours of the stars homes, because I wanted to see where George Clooney lived because he was one of my favorite actors… and single… and everyone knows that your Hollywood crush is just waiting for you to turn up so they can marry you. It's a well-known fact. Google it.

We ran every weekday morning on the bike path, the best part of which was we got to watch the sun rise together. We window shopped on the Third Street Promenade. We swam in the ocean at least once a week. And we made love in every room of his condo and on every piece of furniture he had. Life was good.

Then one night at the end of the month, we sat on the patio eating the salmon we'd grilled, and Jag told me that he'd be leaving to go to Glendale, Arizona, for spring training the week before Valentine's Day. I was shocked. I'd forgotten about spring training, and when he told me he'd be gone for more than six weeks, my mouth hung open.

"Sorry, baby. I thought you knew."

"I-I, uh, did!" I sputtered. Duh. My brothers would've been so ashamed of me at that moment. How could I have forgotten? Duh again.

"I'll be back home end of March or first of April." He cupped my face and rubbed his thumb over my cheek.

"O-okay," I replied, my head still whirling from the information I'd so stupidly forgotten.

"You'll be fine here, right?"

"Yeah! Oh, yeah, it's all good. You go get ready to be a star," I replied with a smile.

"I'll definitely try," he said grinning back at me.

I knew I'd be fine when he left. I was settled into my class schedule, the labs kept me busy, we were getting ready to work with cadavers (ick), so I knew that although I'd miss him like crazy, I'd be focused on school and it'd make being without him for a month and a half easier to take.

One evening as I was walking out of the condo—I was dressed in a Dodgers hoodie, my ripped-at-the-knees jeans, and had my ponytail pulled through a Dodgers cap, totally a walking billboard for my boyfriend's team—I had my head down since I was texting Rebecca, and I all but ran into a gorgeous woman who was coming up the walk.

"Oh! I'm so sorry!" I said. When I looked up, I had another jaw-dropping moment in less than a month as I recognized her as one of those underwear models for a lingerie store. Holy shit, she was stunning.

"It's okay," she said with a sexy accent as she smiled at me.

"D-do you live here?" I asked, smiling back, totally fangirling over this chick.

"Yes. In number 248."

Number 248… just down the hall from Jag's condo. Hm. "Oh, cool. So how long have you lived here?"

"For about a year. I usually come here when we have a beach shoot. But I also have places in Brazil and New York, so I'm not here a lot. Which condo is yours?"

"Number 243."

She thought for a second before her eyes lit up. "Oh! The sexy American baseball player, right?"

"Right," I answered, now narrowing my eyes at her suspiciously.

"I told my agent that he and I should do some commercials together. We'd be so hot together," she said with a giggle.

"Right," I repeated. Is it possible to be enthralled with someone while at the same time you just want to stab them in the eye?

"Are you his sister?" *Sister* came out as *seester* and it sounded beautiful and I totally *needed* to stab her in the eye then just for the fact that she hadn't even presumed that Jag and I were together.

"No, I'm his girlfriend." I kept my eyes narrowed at her, sizing her up. She was around five foot ten and weighed maybe a buck fifteen. I was pretty sure I could take her.

"Oh," she said, looking me up and down with a shitty smirk on her face as if she'd found me lacking.

"Well, it was nice meeting you," I lied. "I was heading to the grocery store," I said, turning to go.

"Is your baseball player home? My car was making a noise and I wondered if he could take a look at it again. He did one time before when he was alone." Her eyes now sparkled wickedly at me as she smiled, which made her cheekbones so beautiful and pronounced and I wanted to stab her in them too. I thought back to Thanksgiving when Jag had said he'd feel a lot better when I moved out here. I wondered if that was because he'd been tempted by her... Oh, who was I fooling? He was a red-blooded, American male. *Of course* he'd been tempted. Ugh.

And seriously? This chick could probably have George Clooney, so why'd it seem as if she was challenging me with Jag? Not that Jag wasn't as hot, if not hotter, than Clooney, but this woman could probably have any man she wanted. I let out a breath and looked out at the parking lot to see some fancy, little red convertible that probably cost a mint and I was sure there was nothing wrong with it.

"No, he's not home. Sorry." I started moving down the walk to my car wanting to get away from her and her superior looks.

"What was your name?" she hollered after me.

I glanced back at her, all perfect in her skinny jeans and heels and blouse that was opened to show her cleavage, her long, beautiful, highlighted brown hair flowing so lovely around her face, past her shoulders, and sighed, sure that she wanted to laugh at my outfit and it was obvious she felt threatened by me not one little bit. "Ellen."

"Ellen." Then she humphed. She humphed at my name! What a bitch. "I'm Alessandra. It was nice meeting you," she said on a hair flip and with another gorgeous smile, turned and model-walked her way to her condo, leaving me standing there feeling like the ugly, illegitimate child of Keith Richards and Steven Tyler.

Now, I didn't think that I had self-esteem issues, I'd always felt pretty good about myself, but I'd bet that any woman who ran into someone who looked like *that* and that woman knew that the woman looking like *that* had been around her man… alone… would have felt the same way I was feeling right then.

I got in my car, started it and took off, all the while mumbling, "Ales*sand*ra" the way she'd said her name. God, even her name was beautiful and just saying it made *me* want to flip *my* hair back.

"Hey, babe, how're things going in PT land?" Jag asked that night when he called.

"They're good. How're things going in ST land?"

"Good. Got my arm on ice right now. Threw around thirty pitches today. Haven't thrown that much in a while, so I'm dragging a little."

"Dang. You're a damned workhorse."

"Yep. That's me," he said with a chuckle.

"So… I met our neighbor today."

"Oh yeah?"

"Yep." I couldn't help but pop the *P*, having gotten a little pissed off the more I thought of Jag checking out Ales*sand*ra's car for her.

There was silence for a couple seconds until he asked, "You gonna tell me which one?"

"I'll give you a hint. Little, red sports car. Legs up to her flippin' neck."

I heard him clear his throat. "Oh. So you met Alessandra?"

"Yeahhhhhh." I drew that out about three seconds too long. I didn't want to come off as the jealous girlfriend, but give me a break here.

"Babe."

"Don't you 'babe' me, Jagger Knox Jensen."

"El, she was coming back from the beach and she asked me to loo—"

"Wait." Dear God. If she'd been in a fucking bikini I was *so* seriously gonna stab the cow now. "She was coming back from the *beach*?"

"Uh, yeah."

"Jag. I'd like to think that I have a pretty good handle on who I am. But when it comes to an *underwear model coming back from the beach* then asking *my boyfriend* to help with her car that I *know* there wasn't a goddamned thing wrong with, then I tend to get just a little irritated!"

"El, calm down, baby."

"Is *she* the reason when, at Thanksgiving, you said you needed me out here?"

I could hear him sigh into the phone. Was I wrong to argue about this? I mean, really, was I? Besides, Mom always said that sometimes couples have to argue to be reminded that their love's worth fighting for. Yeah, I'd go with that excuse.

"The reason I said I needed you was because I fucking needed you."

Oh.

Well, now I felt like a first-class bitch. He hadn't been gone for even a week and I was already ripping into him. Yay me.

It was my turn to sigh. "I'm sorry, Jag. It's just that she's… well, she's beautiful. I got a little jealous, I guess."

Lame. I was so lame.

"El, if I wanted anyone else, don't you think I'd have found someone else by now?"

Well, that wasn't very nice. My hackles rose on that little pronouncement. And, by golly, two could play that game. So, stupid, stupid me antied up and went for it. "Same here, Jag. There've been lots of opportunities that I could've taken, but I've always chosen you." (Can I use the excuse that I was only twenty-one and that's why my maturity level was lacking? Didn't think so. Damn.)

I swear a blast of cold air hit me smack dab in the face from my phone's receiver.

"Jag?" I whispered.

"All you gotta do is say the word, El."

Huh? What word? Idiot? As in "I'm an"?

"I don't know what you're saying, Jag."

I heard him sigh again and I knew he was rubbing his hand over his face. "You don't wanna be with me, just say the word."

"That's not what I'm saying, Jag. I said I'm sorry. I told you I got a little jealous. What you said hurt my feelings, so I reacted like a five year old. End of."

"Nothing to be jealous of, El. Did you talk to Alessandra at all? She's a bitch. If I wanted a bitch, I'd be with one. *End of.*"

Uh oh. Hateful, sarcastic Jag was never a good thing. But at least he'd seen through her big-boob-gorgeous-hair-make-every-man-in-the-entire-world-lust-after-her-super-dee-duper-model façade. And that totally didn't make me feel much better.

"I said I was sorry…"

"I know. Look, you're tired, I'm tired. Let's call it a night. I'll talk to you tomorrow, okay?"

"Okay. Jag?"

"Yeah?"

"I love you."

"Forever and a day, babe. 'Night."

"Good night, Jag."

We hung up and I went outside to sit on the patio and cried. In all the time Jag and I had been apart, at least I had someone else around, but now I had no one. I was completely alone. And lonely. Guess I could've asked Ms. Fabulous herself to hang out, but I'd had enough bitchiness for the evening and didn't want to add hers to mine.

Waiting at the airport for Jag, I proudly held up the bedazzled-with-silver-glitter-and-multicolored-rhinestones sign that I'd made that said "Mr. Jensen" on it. I knew that when he saw it, he'd roll his eyes at me, but I was so excited to see him and I wanted him to know that I'd missed him enough that I was willing to utilize my limited art skills.

I stood amidst a slew of reporters who held microphones, checking with their cameramen to make sure the lighting was just right, photographers ready to snap pictures left and right of their beloved Dodgers arriving back from spring training, and hoped my silly little sign would draw his attention.

It'd been a long almost two months to say the least. The good news was that I'd made some friends at school and had also met Mr. Ashton across the hall and the Lenoxes who were down the hall had invited me for dinner one night, so I hadn't been as lonely as I was when Jag first left, thank God. I think I would've gone stir crazy if my social life, if that's what you wanted to call it, hadn't taken off.

Mr. Ashton was a sweetheart who'd asked for help with his groceries one day and had given me a standing invitation to have coffee with him mornings whenever I felt so inclined. I'd gone over a couple times, but his fifty-five cats, okay, he didn't really have that many... so, his fifty-*four* cats had made my allergies act up and I'd ended up leaving both times with watery, red eyes and sneezing my face off. To make sure I didn't hurt his feelings, I was going to have to either plan my visits farther apart or have him over to our place to avoid all the dander.

The Lenoxes were one of the nicest couples I'd ever met. They reminded me of Jag's parents a lot. Mrs. Lenox, Amber, was the motherly type just like Mary, and she'd even brought me some homemade chicken noodle soup when my allergies had flared up. Mr. Lenox, Al, had made sure to check on me daily since he knew Jag was gone.

When I saw Jag coming into the concourse, my heart practically skipped a beat. The man seriously got better looking each time I saw him. And that walk of his. Good God. The way he carried himself was so damned sexy, his long strides smoothly moving him forward so easily. I saw that he'd kept the scruff and I couldn't agree more that it was a good look for him. Gah! My boyfriend was freaking hot!

As our eyes met, I saw a flicker of wickedness in his as if he couldn't wait to get me alone, which was *way* okay by me. He picked up his pace before a sassy little female reporter jumped in front of him, immediately sticking her microphone in his face as the cameraman did the same with his camera, halting Jag's progress toward me. A look of surprise appeared on his face at first, which made me giggle, but as she asked him question after question and he grew more comfortable as he answered, he looked like a real pro as he laughed a couple times with her, and my chest swelled with pride.

When his interview ended, he resumed his original course, heading toward me, but then another reporter jumped in his path, halting his progress once again. And this pattern went on for at least thirty more minutes. No lie. My guy was famous!

I ended up taking a seat in the waiting area and called Jag's mom to tell her what was going on. She was so excited to know that he was getting so much attention from the press. Then she started crying which made me start crying, so there I sat in an airport blubbering like crazy. A sweet older woman came over and handed me a couple tissues, and I thanked her through broken sobs.

I'd hung up with Mrs. Jensen and was dabbing at my eyes when Jag finally broke away from the madness.

"That for me?"

I looked up and saw him standing in front of me as he jerked his head toward the sign I'd put in the seat beside me.

I nodded and started crying again before jumping up and wrapping my arms around his neck. His arms laced around my waist and he twirled me around while burying his face in my hair and mumbling, "God, I've missed you."

"I've missed you too," I said through my tears when he set me down.

"Baby," he said with a smile, wiping my tears away with his thumbs as he cupped my face in his hands. Then he leaned down and laid a hot, wet one on me as the cameras flashed away. Yikes.

"Jag," I whispered, pulling away and looking around at the reporters watching us as they scribbled away on notepads.

"Guess I'm famous now, El. Get used to it," he said with an eyebrow waggle, chuckling as he continued holding my face, looking down at me like I was the best thing he'd ever seen.

And I loved that.

I tiptoed up and kissed him, not caring one bit that more flashes went off. "Hey, it's kinda like *Beauty and the Beast*," I said with a chuckle pulling back and looking around at all the flashes.

He snorted. "I guess so. See? Fireworks. Stick with me, babe, and that's what you'll get." He wrapped an arm around my shoulders, bent to pick up the sign I'd made for him, looked at it nodding in approval then said, "Let's go get my luggage," as he led me to the baggage claim area.

On his knees behind me, I was on my hands and knees on the bed in front of him, Jag clutched the headboard with one hand, his other arm wrapped around me, holding me to him tightly, his chest against my back, as he showed me how much he'd missed me. And, oh my, had he missed me.

When we'd gotten back from the airport, we'd barely made it inside the condo before practically tearing off each other's clothes, our lips mashing together heatedly before he picked me up, making his way to the bedroom. Once there, his knee hit the bed and he came down on top of me, lifted my hips with his hands then slammed inside me so hard and so fast, my body tensed and I came immediately, my neck arching up as I cried out his name.

"Fuck yeah," he now growled as he pumped inside me roughly.

This act wasn't sweet, it wasn't tender, but it was perfect.

"Missed you, babe," he breathed huskily in my ear .

God, I loved when he got carried away, so turned on that he made me feel that I was all he needed.

"Missed you too, Jag," I panted. His chest, slick with sweat, slid against my back.

He groaned and his hand that was on the headboard hit the bed as his thrusts sped up, becoming more powerful, his hips driving into mine hard several times before he buried himself to the hilt with a grunt. His forehead came down to rest on my shoulder and his arm around my chest pulled me even more tightly to him. We were both breathing heavily when he turned, pulling me with him, to lie on his back, my head landing on his outstretched arm.

"Jesus," he mumbled, his chest still rising and falling rapidly.

"Yeah," I mumbled right back, breathing just as hard as he was as we lay there staring at the ceiling.

Jag was uber busy that season, playing almost two hundred games by the time October came around. Well, he didn't pitch every game, but, of course, he had to be at them. I'd gone to almost every home game but didn't travel with him. I did fly to Chicago at the end of April when they played the Cubs, getting there Friday afternoon and staying the weekend, splitting my time between both our parents' houses and Rebecca's apartment. Jag knew I missed everyone, so he gave me the plane ticket as an early birthday present, which thrilled me to death. He kind of figured that out when I jumped on him, knocking him to the living room floor and proceeded to kiss him fifty bazillion times. He'd also gotten tickets for everyone, his family, my family, my brothers included, and Rebecca and Ross to go to the game with me, and I don't think he was too embarrassed when Rebecca and I made our entire crew do the wave when he took the mound.

As the season went along, I'd gotten to know several of the wives and girlfriends of the players, and for the most part they were all pretty nice. One of the outfielder's wives, Gwen, was a real sweetheart who clued me in on everything. She and I sat together every home game in the seats behind home plate that were reserved for wives and girlfriends. We'd exchanged numbers and had hung out together a couple times when our guys were on the road. She worked at a boutique in Beverly Hills and when I'd gone by to see her one day, she told me she could get me some really good deals by using her discount if I found anything I liked. I'd had to laugh when I picked up a Fendi handbag I liked and saw the price, which even if I were to use her discount, the thing would still have cost over a thousand bucks. Good grief. I told her I'd pass for now, which made her laugh too.

The team ended up finishing third in their division, which meant their season was over, which was disappointing, but it also meant I'd get to see Jag more. That is until his agent, Dirk Dixon, started getting endorsement deals for him. Now, I was all for supporting Jag's career. I loved that he was already semi-famous and well on his way to super stardom, but it seemed that ol' Dirk was all for keeping us apart for some reason.

I'd met Dirk at a party one of the players had thrown at the beginning of the season, and although he was a nice enough guy, I got a strange feeling about him. I guess that feeling could've come from the fact that every time I looked around, he seemed to be watching me. I didn't know what that was all about, I'd even told Jag about it (he just laughed it off) but the guy still gave me the creeps. He reminded me of Jerry Maguire a lot—good looking, around six-feet tall, athletic build, in his early thirties and he was a true schmoozer. I decided to trust Jag's judgment when it came to Dirk, but that didn't mean I wasn't going to keep an eye on him.

As soon as the season was officially over, Dirk began booking all kinds of gigs for Jag, which was truly a good thing. The first commercial he contracted had Jag promoting pickup trucks at a local car dealership. A local insurance company hired him next. These were cool but pretty small jobs, but when Dirk secured a Nike endorsement for Jag, we were absolutely ecstatic. That was big. Huge. Afterward I thought maybe Dirk wasn't so bad.

Chapter 16

I was twenty-two when things got a little shaky between Jag and me.

We flew home to Chicago for Thanksgiving right after Jag had done some ads for Nike. My brothers, of course, had to rib him a little for looking like a pretty boy, which Jag took good-naturedly. We also went home for Christmas, and I was glad we got to see our families over both holidays.

After New Year's, things settled back down, with me attending school as usual and Jag dividing his time with going to his trainer, attending team meetings and learning to surf some more. He even got me out there a couple times, but I didn't have the surfing bug, so I left it up to him. I just didn't have great patience with falling time and time again. Into freezing cold water. That was salty. And possibly contained sharks.

When spring training came around again, Jag took off for Glendale on a definite high since he'd just finished shooting another ad for Nike. I was so proud of him. We'd bought the current *Sports Illustrated* that featured the ad that had him sitting on a weight bench "sweating," curling a dumbbell and all decked out in everything Nike. His arm muscles were bulging as he lifted the weight and he looked hot! While he was gone, I had the ad and the cover of the magazine framed for him in a big poster frame and hung it over the fireplace to surprise him when he got home.

Things were pretty much the same as they'd been the year before when he was gone, with Mr. Ashton and me setting up weekly coffee dates—I had him over to our place this go 'round since he'd added a couple more kitty allergy assassins to his mix and I didn't want a repeat of last year's oh-so-fun reaction to them. The Lenoxes still kept an eye on me too. Al fixed my garbage disposal once and we all had dinner together several times over the course of Jag's absence. I hadn't seen Alessandra since the previous spring. I guessed she'd probably been on location on some tropical island having pictures taken of her gorgeous body. That or she'd had a tragic thong accident which involved the words *anal* and *surgery*. Hey, one can dream.

Right after Jag had left for spring training I'd gotten a job at one of the Starbucks in town, only working a couple days a week. Jag was paying all the bills and I felt like a freeloader, so I thought I'd contribute a little. I'd saved some from my previous job so I did have some cash available, but I also found that I got bored pretty easily when he was gone, being able to study only so much, so it kept me occupied and broke up the ennui some.

When spring training ended, Jag was again busy as all get out, playing games and endorsing even more products that Dirk had booked for him to promote. I had to admit, a small perk of Jag's being gone to spring training was that I didn't have to deal with Dirk. Even though he'd moved up a notch or two on my "Meh" scale, I still had a strange feeling about the guy.

School was keeping me busy as I was having either practicals, exams or quizzes at least once a week, sometimes all three. Talk about stressful. But I still made it to a lot of Jag's home games, and I'd even gotten to go to one of his video shoots for a commercial he and another player were doing for a cell phone company, which was fascinating to watch how it was made. It was also a pretty cute ad that was about dropped calls of other companies, and they used a phone as the ball that Jag had to pitch then the other player, an outfielder, dropped it. Corny, but cute.

Gwen and I still sat together at the games, and we tried calling each other when the team was out of town to make plans to shop or get lunch, but I was getting really busy with school so that most of the time I'd had to pass.

As the semester went along, things became even more hectic and Jag and I hardly saw each other at all, with me missing games because I had to study, and it was even worse if he had back-to-back away games because we'd go weeks at a time not seeing each other. On top of all the games, in his spare time, the tons of endorsement deals that Dirk made sure to book, took up any free time he had.

One evening when he came home from some endorsement gig he'd been working on for the entire week, he walked to the dining table where I was studying and said, "We need to talk."

I looked up at him with a smile, which fell quickly when I saw the look on his face. Crap! What was this about? "Okay…"

He sat down in the chair next to mine, turning it to face me and ran his hands over his face then up through his dark hair, lacing his fingers together and resting his hands on top of his head. God, he was handsome. It always just struck me at some of the weirdest times how good looking he was. Like, I'd look at him after having been hanging out with him for an hour and it'd suddenly just hit me how sexy he was. He'd now made a habit of sporting scruff on his cheeks, which he knew I loved because I'd told him it gave him a really rugged look. His hair was a little longer than he'd ever worn it too, but it looked great on him. And his tan made his glacier blue eyes even more striking surrounded by his thick, black lashes. I sat watching him as he looked anywhere but at me.

"What's wrong?" I asked, suddenly scared to even know.

He glanced at me and took a deep breath, expelling it then brought his hands down, taking mine into them. "This commercial I've been working on?"

"Yeah?"

"I thought at first it was for suntan lotion or something, at least that's what Dirk told me."

"Yeah?"

"It wasn't."

"Okay…"

He bit the inside of his lip and looked down at our hands. Good grief. Just what could be so bad about this?

"It was for swimsuits from the lingerie company Alessandra models for." He looked up at me, watching me closely.

All I'd heard was *swimsuits*, *lingerie* and *Alessandra* and it was enough to make me suck in a deep breath. Then all I could do was just look at him, finally noticing that he was wearing a blue button down that was untucked and unbuttoned halfway down to expose a white wife beater underneath, his sleeves were rolled up to expose his muscular forearms and he had on some pretty fancy faded jeans. He hardly ever wore button down shirts and never wife beaters, spending most of his time in t-shirts like I did. Huh.

"Was Alessandra there?" I asked, remembering back to her little comment about her and Jag doing a commercial together and knowing that she'd probably made it happen by using her sexy, Brazilian voice, cooing in her agent's ear and convincing him to hook them up.

Jag held my hands tighter and I already knew the answer.

"Yeah."

All right. Nothing to be upset about. It wasn't like they'd gone on a date or anything. They'd made a commercial. And I'd attended the cell phone one and saw how technical it all was, so this couldn't have been that big of a deal.

I nodded then said, "Okay."

"Okay?" he asked, surprised that I wasn't ripping him a new one.

"Yeah, okay. I mean, it was a commercial, right? It couldn't have been that bad, could it? I mean, you didn't have to kiss her or anything, did you?" I cringed a little when I said those last two words, not wanting to hear that it *was* that bad.

"No. Nothing like that. It wasn't bad. We filmed on the beach. There were around ten other girls there, so it wasn't like it was just us."

Oh, so now they were an "us." Great. All I could do was sit there and nod stupidly.

"So… you're all right with it?"

"Yeah! I'm fine!" Well, that came out two octaves too high, but it was all I had at the moment. And I wasn't going to be *that* girl—the jealous, whining, bitchy girlfriend who was so insecure that she folded at the news of her hotter-than-hell boyfriend cozying up to the hotter-than-hell supermodel who lived down the hall.

"Good. Thanks for understanding, babe." He leaned in with a smile and kissed my nose then got up, heading toward the bedroom to change his clothes.

I followed him asking where he'd gotten the clothes.

"They provided them for me for the commercial," he explained with a shrug as he took off his boots and socks, unbuttoning the top button of his jeans.

"Cool."

"Yeah."

"Um, so when does this commercial air?" I questioned.

"They said in a couple weeks. I'll probably be in Colorado when it does."

Hm. So he'd thought it through as if he didn't want to be around me when it aired. Good to know. "Oh. Okay."

"Yeah."

Well, weren't we the vocal ones?

"Gotta finish studying for finals," I said, watching as he took off his shirt which left him in the wife beater. Wow. I'd never really liked wife beaters, but, damn, he looked good in it. It clung to his well-defined pecs and tight abs, and it made his shoulder and arm muscles look huge.

"Gonna shower," he said back, looking back at me, his eyes turning that damned navy which made my breathing speed up.

"'Kay," I mumbled, still not leaving the room.

"'Kay," he muttered, walking toward me in his unbuttoned jeans and wife beater. Gah! His hands went to the hem of my t-shirt and he pulled it over my head and off, his eyes glittering down at me when he saw that I didn't wear a bra.

Looking him over, I couldn't keep my hands off, as I ran them up his abs then over his chest and up to his scruffy cheeks, cupping his face and pulling him down to kiss me. His hands went to my hips then slid up and under my breasts where his thumbs smoothed across my nipples. He stepped away from me and quickly pulled his wife beater off, turning it around in his hands and sliding it over my head and on me. I laughed in surprise, but when he growled deep in his throat and grabbed the back of the shirt, twisting it in his hand to make it tighter on me then yanked me closer to him, I gasped before his mouth came down hard on mine. After that, every bit of our clothing came off but the wife beater I wore.

He led me to the bathroom where he pulled me into the shower, making me keep the shirt on as he sprayed water on it. "Goddamn," he muttered, lust flickering in his eyes as he took in my White T-shirt Contest moment, my nipples hard and straining against the thin fabric. His mouth came down hard on mine and he then proceeded to erase any thoughts of his commercial with what's-her-face from my mind.

My cell phone rang one evening in the middle of June when Jag was in Colorado.

"Oh. My. God." Rebecca said indignantly.

"Shit. You saw it."

I heard her take a breath. "El, are you sitting down? Sit down."

Shit! I'd told her about the commercial Jag was in and when it was supposed to air, and since she was two hours ahead of me, I guess it'd shown already. I sat down in the big, cushy chair I'd bought from IKEA with my Starbucks money, throwing my legs over one arm while leaning back against the other and waited on the bad news.

"You sitting?"

"Yeah."

She took another breath before informing me, "El, you are not to watch that commercial."

Wait, what? "Um, what?" I asked sitting up.

"El, I'm telling you, do not watch that fucking commercial."

Oh, God. This was bad. Rebecca only cursed when she was upset. Just great.

"Why? What happens in it?"

"Oh, El, it's not good."

"Jesus," I whispered. "What'd Jag do in it? Fuck Alessandra?"

"All but," she whispered back.

Okay, now I was angry. The past weeks with Jag had been great. He hadn't brought up the commercial again, so I assumed there wasn't anything to it, so I let it be. "Are you fucking shitting me?" I hissed. "What happens in it?"

"You're just gonna have to watch for yourself then, although I advise you don't," she said with a sigh. She told me what station it'd aired on and during what program, so I grabbed the remote and turned to the station immediately.

"I will. I'll call you after. Thanks, Bec."

"Wish I were there to make you a Long Island iced tea," she said. "I think you're gonna need one."

"I've got some wine. Think that'll do the trick?"

"Is it one of those jumbo bottles?"

Oh, boy. This was just fabulous. "No, but I've got three bottles."

"That should do it."

We hung up, I got the wine, downed a glass quickly then poured another, downing it just as fast. Then I sat and waited.

Ever had one of those moments where you knew you were alive and breathing but it felt like every bit of oxygen had left your body as if you'd been punched in the gut? Yep. My gut-punching moment had occurred at exactly nine-oh-eight in the evening when, get this, the Dodgers versus the Rockies game had gone to break.

The regular programming had been preempted by the game. How ironic was that? So I'd been sitting there watching Jag pitch thinking that maybe the commercial wasn't that bad, that Rebecca had just been overly preparing me because I'd told her about Alessandra and she knew the chick just royally chapped my ass. But when I actually saw it, I knew why Rebecca had seriously been concerned for me. And she should've been. Good lord, even having self medicated with several glasses of the White Zinfandel Mrs. Jensen had gotten from the Napa Valley tour and had sent back with us the Christmas before, I still hadn't been prepared.

After seeing the ad, I'd sat there stunned after pausing the DVR, then I'd backed the son of a bitch up and recorded the damned thing so I could watch it again and again, to torture myself to shreds, I supposed.

I restarted and watched again as it showed Jag walking along the beach barefooted, wearing the outfit he'd worn home the night of the filming, as the nine or so models passed by him with their perfect bikini-clad bodies looking at him seductively as he ignored them. Then he looked wistfully out at the waves while flashbacks showed of him and Alessandra rolling around in a bed together and they appeared to be naked.

And that was the moment I thought that I was going to throw up.

But being the masochist that I was, I kept the stupid thing rolling. It next showed him stopping as he looked out at the ocean as if he'd seen something. The following scene was then of Alessandra appearing out of the waves like she was some kind of sea goddess and walking toward him with a sexy smile on her face, wearing a bikini that barely covered her fucking tits or ass at all. After her slow motion approach that showed plenty of slomo boob jiggling, she ended up running to Jag where he swept her up in his arms, twirling her around as they looked longingly into each other's eyes. The camera then started panning back showing him setting her down, their bodies still melded together, her arms wrapped around his neck, his hands going to her face as he leaned down as if to kiss her. And even though he'd said they hadn't, you really couldn't tell if they'd kissed because the back of his head was to the camera, and by then it'd panned farther away while some guy said something and some words flashed on the screen, all of which I paid no attention to.

"Oh, God," I whispered then ran to the bathroom and emptied my stomach of all the wine I'd drunk.

Aside from the obvious, one of the worst moments of all was when programming went back to the game and the announcers went on and on about the commercial and what a lucky man Jag was to have gotten to work with Alessandra, that she was a gorgeous woman, and that they hoped he didn't have a wife or girlfriend because they'd be green with envy right about now.

While I was in the bathroom washing out my mouth, my phone rang. I walked into the living room and picked it up, knowing it was Rebecca.

"Oh, God, Bec. What the fuck was that?" I asked.

"I don't know, babe. I wish I could tell you, though."

Okay, I had to be rational. Jag was young. He was new to all of this, so he'd probably just followed along with what the director had told him, not realizing how graphic it'd been, or if he had, he probably felt as if he couldn't really say anything. I guess it really wasn't that graphic but for the fact that Alessandra was topless in the bed (bitch!), but to me, his girlfriend of five years, it had been particularly licentious. But I had to give him the benefit of the doubt. Didn't I?

"Bec, I've gotta be rational here," I told her.

"You don't have to be anything but pissed, El," she replied.

"Well, I am that, but Jag's no pro at this stuff. I mean, he was probably just taking direction and doing what they told him to do."

"Maybe," she capitulated grudgingly.

"I'll just have to talk to him about it and see what he has to say after he watches it."

"Yeah, do that and then let me know what he has to say for himself," she snapped.

I knew she was angry for me and that's what a best friend should do, but I also knew that Jag wouldn't willingly have hurt me, so I'd just wait and see what he said.

"Thanks for being such a good friend, Bec. I'm glad I've got you on my side," I told her.

"Same, El. I'm here for you always and I understand what you're saying," she said. "But that doesn't mean I don't want to beat the shit out of both of them."

I chuckled at that then we talked a bit more before hanging up. I didn't turn the TV back on that night. I didn't have one shit left to give about Jag's game and I damn sure didn't want to risk seeing that godforsaken commercial again. When he called the next day, I'd get my answers. I went to bed, hoping I'd been right about everything.

Jag didn't call the next two days. I then knew that he knew that I knew. And I knew that he didn't want to get into it over the phone. Smart man.

In the meantime, my mom had called, Jag's mom had called, and my brother Robbie had called, and he was pissed as all hell. I talked with each of them, telling them my take on it, that Jag was inexperienced and had probably been coerced into the whole thing, and that seemed to settle everyone down. Well, except for Robbie. Before we'd hung up, he told me that he didn't give a fuck who Jag was, that the next time he saw him, he was going to beat the shit out of him. Alrighty then.

The day Jag was due home, he'd texted to let me know he'd be in around seven that night. I texted back that I had to work until ten so I'd see him when I got home and that was all we'd said. Gee, no tension was building between us at all. Ugh.

When I left for work that afternoon, I noticed Alessandra's little, red car parked in the lot, and my mind immediately went into Chick Think mode as I envisioned all kinds of scenarios: Jag had called to let her know he'd be home too, that I wouldn't be home until later and they could have a tryst while I was out. Or I'd walk in the door after hours of barista'ing my ass off to find them entangled in each other's arms, naked in our bed of course, and they'd explain that they were only practicing for their next commercial. Or they were running off together and would I mind so much moving out as soon as possible.

By the time I got home, I needed a Xanax. I swear Chick Think was the damned bane of my existence.

"Breathe. Stay focused. Be open-minded. And whatever you do, do *not* stab anyone," I muttered to myself as I walked toward the condo door. Before putting the key in the lock, I pressed my ear to the door to see if I could hear any telltale sounds of bumping and grinding going on, but all I heard was the TV. And that was when Jag decided to open the door and I all but fell into his arms.

"Whoa, baby. What're you doing?" he asked, looking down at me with his half grin. That damned sexy grin that always made me want to kiss his face off, but I wasn't falling for it this time. Not until I had some answers.

"Whoops. These darn shoes, always tripping me up," I mumbled, looking down at my cute little black biker shoes that in no way had hindered my balance.

"Mm hm." He narrowed his eyes at me as he pulled me inside. "I missed you," he said as he leaned down to kiss me, but I dodged it, moving out from under his arms and into the living room, heading toward the bedroom.

"Missed you too," I said flippantly over my shoulder, before entering the bedroom and toeing off my shoes, proceeding to untuck my polo shirt. I was pretty proud of myself with how I was handling things. I thought surely I'd be more nervous when I saw him, but I was owning this shit. I pulled my hair tie out, taking down my ponytail then reached inside the dresser drawers to grab some underwear, a t-shirt and shorts but upon turning to make my way to the shower, I let out a squeak when I ran right into a brick wall, which would be Jag's broad chest.

"Hey," he said, his finger going under my chin to lift my face to his. His brows were drawn down in concern as he looked at me. "El…"

I looked away as I said, "Jag, I need to shower. I worked all day long. I smell like a giant cappuccino."

He let out a deep sigh then finally said, "Go." So I went. And he left the room.

Well, what'd he expect? That I'd be thrilled that he'd practically made out with our supermodel neighbor? And the entire nation saw it, including our families and friends? That would be a negative. I mean, if the situation were reversed, he'd have thrown a tantrum.

After washing the dregs of work off my body and mentally giving myself a productive pep talk, I was ready to face him and walked into the living room. He'd been watching a ballgame, but turned the TV off the minute he saw me. "You hungry?"

"A little."

"I got In-N-Out Burger while you were in the shower," he said, raising his eyebrows expectantly at me.

Well, damn. He was trying to butter me up, and I had to admit he was doing a good job of it. Of all the fancy restaurants we'd eaten at in the area, I'd take In-N-Out Burger over all of them any day. Their burgers were fantastic and the root beer floats were to die for.

"You sit down. You've been on your feet all day." He guided me to the dining table, pulling out a chair for me then went into the kitchen to retrieve my food. "I got you a float too."

After he placed everything in front of me, I thanked him and dug in. I'd been so upset the past few days, I guess I'd forgotten to eat, which showed by the way I'd begun stuffing my face.

He watched me the entire time, pleased with himself, I could tell, that he'd gotten me something I liked. Whatever. I was starving, the food was amazing, and I didn't really care about anything else right then.

When I finished, I thanked him again then we sat there in silence, well, mostly silence as my slurps of my float filled the room, until he got up and cleared my place then came back to me, lifting me out of my chair then sitting in it himself and placing me sideways on his lap. "Let's talk."

"Do I have much choice?" I asked.

He chuckled. "No, you don't." He curled a piece of hair over my ear. "I'm sorry, baby."

"For?"

"For the, uh, commercial."

"You don't sound too sorry."

"I am. I didn't realize it would hurt your feelings that much. Mom called and griped me out." He looked at me sheepishly.

I sighed. He didn't realize his rolling around in a bed with a half-naked woman would hurt my feelings that much? "Are you dense?"

He pulled back with a jerk and a frown on his face. "Am I dense? What's that supposed to mean?"

God, he really was that dense. I set my float down and jumped off his lap afraid I'd smack him if I sat there any longer then I started pacing. "Jag, really?"

"Really, what?"

I stopped and glared at him. Damn. He really didn't get it. "Remember back to a party a couple years ago? Does the name Slade mean anything to you?"

He narrowed his eyes at me as a scowl formed on his face.

"Ring a bell?" I asked snottily.

"Yeah, it does. Your point?" he snapped.

"You drove thirteen hours because it pissed you off seeing me in pictures with him. Pictures where he and I had only hugged and were just talking. How angry do you think you would've been if you'd been sent video of us rolling around naked in bed together? Huh?" My voice had risen, but it always tended to do that when I was trying to get a point across to someone who just didn't get it. I'd thrown in the arm flail for good measure hoping I'd get through to him.

He sat there for a minute and then it was like the damned light bulb had finally come on. Thank God. "But, El, it was just for a commercial. And I didn't kiss her."

Wow. "You don't get it, Jag. And it's the principle of it all. Something to do with respect for me!" I shouted, shaking my head.

"I do get it, but it's not that big of a deal, El!" he shouted right back.

"Are you shitting me?" I all but screamed. He so totally just didn't *get* it. Argh!

"Keep your voice down," he hissed.

"Why? Afraid Ales*san*dra might hear us and think you're a bad guy?" He just stared up at me not saying a word. "That's it. I'm outta here." I spun to leave, so done with it all.

Jag could move pretty fast when he wanted to. Before I knew it, he'd gotten up, bent down and stuck his shoulder in my stomach, picking me up fireman style and carrying me to the bedroom where he threw me down on the bed. I bounced once before he was on top of me, pinning me down with his body. I bucked underneath him, kicking my legs not wanting to be there, my hands going to his shoulders as I tried pushing him off me. He grabbed my wrists in one hand, pulling them over my head and held them there.

"You're not going anywhere until we get this shit worked out," he snarled.

Now, I didn't really think he had a right to be snarling at the moment. I was the hurt party in this scenario not him. I should be the snarler in this situation, damn it.

"Let me up!" I yelled, kicking my legs some more until he maneuvered a leg over them, stopping any movement.

"Not until you calm down." He was looking at me in shock like I was crazy which didn't help at all. I know he'd never seen me this mad, so I probably did look a little nuts.

I was breathing hard, still trying to get loose, angrier than I'd ever been in my life while he held me down just looking at the wacko chick underneath him and that's when I started crying. Shit.

"Baby," he said.

"Get off me," I sobbed.

He started to loosen his hold on my wrists, but when he felt me tense up as if I'd use my hands to push him away again, he tightened his hold. And that made me cry even harder. In my defense, I hadn't cried about the stupid commercial at all, so I guessed it'd all built up and now the dam had broken.

"El…"

"Please, Jag…"

"Not letting you leave, babe."

Oh. My. God. I was so fucking angry I wanted to claw his eyes out. I closed my own eyes then, appalled that I'd even have those thoughts about him, but he'd cornered me and given me no choice.

"S-swear t-to G-God, if y-you d-don't get o-off m-me, I'll s-scream," I cried.

His mouth came down hard on mine then, and when he rammed his tongue inside, I surprised myself when a low moan escaped me. I'd always loved Jag's kisses, but this was different. This was hard and demanding. I mean, he'd gotten a little rough with me before, which I loved, but there was always a touch of tenderness behind it. This was angry. This was pissed off. And I was all for it.

When he pulled his mouth away, I bit his bottom lip, holding it in my teeth watching as his deep, blue eyes glittered back at mine as if to say, "You really wanna go there?" When I didn't let his lip go right away, he got my answer loud and clear, knowing I'd accepted the challenge.

He jerked my t-shirt up with his one hand, baring my breasts to him, his head came down, and he took my nipple in his mouth, sucking hard, making me gasp and arch up off the bed. He moved to my other breast, doing the same thing, and got the same reaction from me. His hand snaked down, going inside my shorts then he roughly pushed his finger inside me.

"Dripping wet. Jesus, El," he hissed, taking my mouth with his once again, pressing down hard and bruising my lips as he pumped his finger inside me. He then removed his hand from my shorts and tugged them and my panties down and off my legs. I heard something rip, but I couldn't have cared less at that moment. His hand went to the fly of his jeans, he grabbed my leg behind the knee drawing my leg up, and I felt the tip of him at my entrance before he rammed inside powerfully making us both cry out.

He still held my hands above my head, and I arched my back up against him, trying to get him to let them go. I wanted to touch him, but God, at this angle, his thrusting so hard inside me was driving me mad.

He felt me spasm around him, knowing I was moving toward a climax. "That's it, baby, I want you to come hard for me," he said huskily in my ear.

"Oh, God," I breathed, knowing I wasn't going to last long.

He let my wrists and leg go then and yanked his shirt off, coming back down on top of me, and that's when things got a little crazy. I brought my knees up to press against his sides and I dragged my nails down his back, scratching the hell out of him, making him suck in a breath and that's when he pulled out and stayed out.

"Don't stop!" I cried. God, I was so close.

"We okay, El?" he asked, looking down at me.

When I didn't answer, just looked back at him not knowing what to say, he slammed back in then pulled out again.

"We okay?"

"I—" When I didn't give him anything else, he executed another punishing slam inside, holding it and grinding into me.

"Baby. We okay?"

"Oh, God," I said all breathy as he ground against me and I felt myself ready to tip over the edge.

His hands slid under me then and he lifted my hips to him, and what I'd thought had been him slamming inside me was nothing compared to what he started doing.

"Gonna make you feel me for days," he said between thrusts so hard and deep that I made a mewling noise each time he entered me.

It only took a few more of these mind-blowing thrusts before we both reached our peak together, which had never happened before and I was kind of in awe of it all. He collapsed on top of me, crushing me, but I didn't mind, loving how he felt on top of me, as he buried his nose in the side of my neck.

We lay that way for several minutes before he pulled back, looking down at me and soberly asked, "Are we okay, El?"

I nodded, a small smile on my face and he bent to kiss me so lovingly, it brought tears to my eyes. He got up to get a washrag, pulling his jeans back over his hips and I gasped when I saw what my nails had done to his back, so ashamed, knowing I'd done it specifically to hurt him. While I lay there, a sob choked out of me because I knew I'd just lied to him. The only way we'd be okay was if he understood why what he'd done bothered me. And I was scared that that wasn't going to happen any time too soon.

When I left for my run the next morning, there stood Alessandra at her car, yelling into her phone blasting someone in Portuguese. She hung up with a huff then looked up and saw me, giving me one of her gorgeous smirks.

"Why hello, Ellen."

"Hi, Alessandra."

"So, I'm sure you've seen the commercial by now. What did you think?"

"It was okay," I answered with a shrug.

"Well, I just want to thank you for loaning me your handsome man for a few days."

"No problem," I said with a sigh.

"We should get together for some girl talk over drinks soon. You can give me some, what do you say? Dimensions. Because from what I felt when he and I were in bed together, your baseball player is very well endowed indeed," she said with a giggle. "I'm just disappointed that I didn't get to find out if his lips are as soft as they look."

I glared at her knowing she was just trying to make me jealous, which she'd absolutely succeeded in doing, but I wouldn't let her get to me. I said goodbye, telling her I had to get to the bike path and took off in a jog. I honestly don't know how I left there without being arrested for assault, but I did. I probably should've been taken in for assault on myself since I ran eight miles at almost a straight sprint. As I walked back to the condo, hands on top of my head, sucking wind like none other, I focused on the one thing that I held onto from the entire conversation I'd just had with Alessandra. It was the fact that Jag hadn't lied to me about kissing her, because I swore, if that'd been the case, and he had actually lied, I'd have been on the next plane back to Chicago.

Chapter 17

I was twenty-three when Jag broke me. Just plain broke me.

A few weeks later, we sat in Dirk's office waiting for him to end the phone call he'd taken right as we'd walked in. He'd asked Jag to meet with him about more endorsements he'd been negotiating, telling him that he wanted me to be there too, for some reason. Jag said it was probably so I'd know what all was coming up and that Dirk was trying to include me more in Jag's professional life too. And wasn't that so kind of him?

As I listened to Dirk schmoozing his way through his call, it was all I could do to keep from rolling my eyes. He was such a fake. He'd say something to whoever he was talking to then look at Jag and me and shake his head, rolling his own eyes like the person was a complete idiot. I looked at Jag with a raised eyebrow, wanting him to realize that Dirk probably did that when he talked to him, but Jag just grinned back at me, totally blind to what kind of sycophantic phony his agent was.

When he finally hung up, Dirk turned to us and apologized for the interruption, mumbling something about how hockey players were such catered-to babies at which he gave a ridiculously fake laugh. Ugh. This guy just totally creeped me out.

"Well, Jagger, I've been talking to the producer and he's ready to move forward."

"Okay," Jag replied with a nod.

I wondered what they were talking about, but was sure I'd soon find out. I had to admit it was somewhat fascinating listening to Dirk, telling us how he'd made this deal or that deal for Jag. The guy was good at his job, that was for sure, but the way he kept smiling at me like he had a big secret made me grit my teeth.

"So, we'll be shooting out at Malibu again, for part two of our little mermaid story," he said looking at me with a smarmy grin.

What the hell? While things hadn't been totally resolved between Jag and me over the commercial, he'd told me that he understood (finally) where I was coming from. He said he wasn't doing any more ads with Alessandra as far as he knew. He also told me that he'd talked to Dirk about it, and Dirk had promised he'd be more discriminating when it came to Jag's endorsements in the future.

"I thought you weren't going forward with this," I said with a frown looking first at Jag then Dirk.

"We're locked in. It's a three-part deal. Jag signed the contract, so the deal's sealed. Sorry," he said insincerely, looking at me with false sympathy. "Guess you'll just have to put up with your boyfriend making love to a beautiful mermaid for a couple more months," he said with a laugh.

I knew I needed to get out of that office when I started looking around Dirk's desk for a letter opener to stab him with.

When we left, it was all I could do to keep from blowing up at Jag until we got out on the street. "What the fuck, Jag? You lied to me!" I screeched making a few people on the street turn to look at me.

He grabbed me by the shoulders, digging his fingers into them and turned me toward him. "Goddamn it, keep it down, El!" he said in a low voice, looking around to make sure people didn't hear him. He let me go and we walked to the car. "I only told you we weren't doing more shoots because it upset you so much the first time. Look, I'm really sick and fucking tired of arguing about this. It's ridiculous. Alessandra isn't that bad. She's actually been pretty nice the last couple times I've talked to her."

Say what? "And when have you talked to her?" I hissed.

"I've seen her around. This is just business, okay? That's it."

We'd gotten to the car, and I got in not waiting on Jag to open the door for me as he usually did. God, I was tired of arguing over this as much as he was. Maybe I was being a bitch about it all. I just didn't know anymore. But I did know that Jag had lied and that was so not cool.

We rode home in silence, and once we got there, he left immediately, telling me he had a team meeting. Well, this had worked out just great.

I honestly didn't know what to do about everything, so I ended up calling my dad to get his advice.

"Hey, Dad," I said with a sob when he answered his phone.

"Ellen? Is everything okay?"

"I don't know anymore," I said, crying harder.

On top of fighting with Jag, I was also entirely sick of was crying. Oh, and maybe I was a little annoyed at being reduced to entertaining thoughts of violence against Dirk and Alessandra all the time too. Just a little. But I'd cried more in the last two months than I'd cried in my entire life. And a big boo-frickin-hoo to that.

I told my dad what was going on, and since he was a lawyer, he explained to me about contracts and all, which I understood. But on the other part, he told me he didn't think I was being too unreasonable, and that Jag should understand where I was coming from and he shouldn't have lied to me even if he was trying to protect me. That made me feel better, but I knew I couldn't throw any of it in Jag's face because then he'd be mad at my dad.

"I love you, Dad. Thank you. Tell Mom and everyone I send them my love," I told him before hanging up.

I sat there thinking after ending the call. This whole situation was unhealthy. I'd lost over ten pounds since the stupid commercial had aired, my nerves being stretched to the limit. God, I had to get hold of myself. I was a strong, self-assured, independent woman and it was ridiculous that I was letting something like this bring me down. I had to get over myself ASAP. I'd be starting back to school in a little over a month, entering my third, last, and most important year, and I couldn't afford to let anything screw it up.

Jag began filming for the second commercial the next week. He was tired and grouchy because he'd been traveling so much, and I could tell he wasn't particularly thrilled with having to split his time between ball and being on set. Such was the life of a star, I guessed. He'd offered to take me with him a few times to filming, but I made sure that my work schedule always conflicted with his, so, darn, I just couldn't make it. After I'd turned him down several times, he stopped asking.

His shoots took the rest of June, the entire month of July and halfway into August because he'd had tons of away games and the lingerie company and crew had to work around it. I kept my mouth shut and dealt with everything, trying to stay positive even if I had to pretend when I was with him that all was well. "Fake it till you make it," they say (there's that moronic "They" again), and by God I was going to fake it until I proved it true.

School began and I was excited to finally see the light at the end of the tunnel. If things went as expected, I'd get my DPT in the spring and start my clinical residency program right after, and I couldn't wait to get started. I'd worked my ass off to get where I was, had put up with plenty of bullshit along the way, and yet I'd made it this far. Nothing was going to stop me at that point.

By mid-September we were back to our old grind. Jag had games out the wazoo and I had my head crammed so far into my books that Armageddon could've come and I'd have just glanced around at all the madness, given a disinterested "Meh" and gone back to studying.

One thing that I did bring my head out of the books for was when Jag started getting attention not only for his athletic prowess, but for his stunning good looks, by various magazines, celebrity gossip shows and web blogs. *Playgirl* had contacted Dirk, wanting to feature Jag (hopefully, he wouldn't agree to posing naked), he'd been labeled one of the "Top 25 Most GQ Male Athletes" by *GQ* and they'd done a spread on him, which had been really hot because they'd dressed him in a tux and a couple of suits along with several different chic but masculine outfits, and even *Inside Edition* ran a spot over "Jag the Stag" (gag) one evening on its broadcast. And I couldn't disagree with any of them. My man was everything they said and more, and I couldn't have been prouder of him. The only thing that remotely bothered me about it all was they all kept trying to tie him to Alessandra.

And didn't things just keep getting better.

Dirk called around that time, but Jag had gone to pick up some food and had accidentally left his phone on the bar, so when it rang, I answered. Dirk had been surprised that I'd answered, the idiot still not being able to figure out that I lived with Jag and was his girlfriend, but whatever, so he'd left a message with me. The last week of September there was to be a dinner party for the premiere of the next installment of the Sea Hag commercial. Well, Dirk had called it the Mermaid commercial, but again, whatever. Anyway, he said Jag and I were to attend, that it was, of course, black tie, there'd be a red carpet, it was even being broadcast on one of the local stations, and that I needed to have Jag return his call when he got in.

The party wasn't just for the commercial, though. The lingerie company was celebrating making its gazillionth dollar or something like that and it was also the CEO's birthday, so a big celebration was to be had for all. Yay. But even with all the crap that surrounded it, I was actually really looking forward to this gig.

All thoughts Vera Wang, Versace and Valentino went through my head as I pictured the fabulous gown I'd wear.

When Jag returned home, I gave him the message, he returned Dirk's call and upon hanging up, told me with a huge grin that I needed to go shopping for some "fancy duds" as he called them. I jumped on him with a scream, knocking him to the floor in my excitement and showed him how happy I was to buy some couture "duds" for the fete.

He left the next morning headed to DC then they'd move on to Pittsburgh and finish up in Atlanta for a grueling two weeks before heading back to take on the Giants at home. But let me tell you, he had a huge smile on his face thanks to the things I'd done to him the night before as a payback for the dress he was buying me. For once, things seemed to be going well for us. About damned time.

Looking back, I can see where it went wrong for us. But I'm getting ahead of myself. How about I start at the beginning of the end.

I'd gotten my dress, and it was the most beautifully sublime thing I'd ever seen. It was an emerald green corset dress of satin with a slit up to "there" by Versace, and had a strap that went over my right shoulder. I was in designer heaven. And don't forget the shoes. Silver, satiny stilettos by Louboutin. Enough said. I'd made appointments for my hair and nails the morning of the reception and had called everyone I knew to share in my excitement, and those who didn't live in the area were all going to tune in via the Internet to watch. Gwen's squeal of excitement pierced my eardrum before she said she'd be watching live. I'd even told my favorite professor and some of my classmates to tune in to which they'd replied that they wouldn't miss it.

The day of the gala, I'd gone that morning to get my hair and nails done while Jag did some much-deserved surfing. Before

I'd left, he'd put on his body suit, which on some people looked ridiculous, but on him, it showed off every muscle of that fine body of his. He'd laughed at the lurid look I'd given him and shooed me out the door with a roll of his eyes.

It was four by the time I returned home all painted and coiffed to the nines, so I started putting my makeup on since we had to leave by six. Jag had texted saying he'd gone to pick up his tux but he'd be back soon. At a little past five, he came into the bedroom where I'd put on the dress and was inspecting it in the mirror making sure I'd zipped every zipper and there were no bulges or anything marring its appearance. The thing fit like a glove and one false turn of the fabric would make it look like crap. I'd had to have it taken in two times since buying it because I'd still been losing weight, my nerves eating away at me almost daily.

"What do you think?" I asked as he came into the bedroom. When he didn't reply, I looked at him and my stomach instantly knotted at the look on his face. "Jag? What is it?"

He closed his eyes, taking in a deep breath then ran his hands over his face and up through his hair. Uh oh.

"Jag?" He looked devastated as if someone had died. Oh, God! Had someone died? "Jag, you're scaring me. What's wrong? Has someone gotten hurt? Are our families okay?" I was in panic mode by then.

"No, no, baby, nothing like that," he assured me, taking my hands and looking down at me, but the look of desolation hadn't left his face.

"What is it then?" I whispered.

He led me to the bed and sat me down, which wasn't an easy feat with as tight as my dress was. Then he knelt on the floor in front of me still holding my hands. Dear lord, what was he going to tell me?

"Dirk called." He watched me carefully, the sadness on his face just overwhelming.

"Yes?" I asked, wanting to know what had happened.

"He, uh… El…"

I could've sworn he choked up, but I'd never seen Jag cry before so that couldn't be right. I let out a nervous chuckle. "What'd he say, Jag?"

He took another deep breath, his hands holding mine tighter before looking at me with such forlornness I reached out and cupped his jaw. "He, uh, said that I was to go to this thing tonight alone."

I drew my hand back instantly as if it'd been burned. "Wh-what?" All the blood drained out of my face. And there I sat in my lovely Versace gown, Louboutins, hair and makeup done up beautifully staring at him in shock.

"I'm sorry, El. I told him I wasn't going either then, but he said I was contractually bound to attend."

All the breath had been knocked out of me. Not just for the fact that my evening had been ruined, but that I knew Dirk had set this whole thing up just to humiliate me. Wow.

"Baby, I'm so sorry. You look beautiful."

I huffed out a chuckle. Yeah. I'm sure I did.

The next hour became a blur in my mind just like Jag's thirteenth birthday party had after he'd kissed Marie Jackson.

Jag got ready as I undressed, carefully hanging my dress back on its hanger. Putting my shoes back in their box. Wiping all the makeup off my face. Taking the pins out of my hair. I moved in a zombie-like fashion, not paying any particular attention to anything, sure that the hollow feeling inside me was going to eat me alive.

"Baby, I'll only stay for as long as is necessary. Again, I'm so sorry, El."

I looked at him all dapper in his tux, just like on Prom night (damn my memory) but I couldn't find it in me to tell him that he looked nice. Autopilot was my friend right then, and all I could do was go through the motions. Before I realized it, he'd left.

I don't know if it's inside everyone, but I'd learned since the commercial aired that I have this little masochistic streak that needs to be fed every so often, and because of this, I tuned into the broadcast of the party. I'd called everyone I could to let them know what'd happened and they'd all commiserated with me which just made me feel worse.

Sitting in my big IKEA chair, my legs thrown over one arm, I drank straight from the bottle of Macallans that Jag had gotten for his last birthday from one of his teammates, watching the damned gala live. If I wasn't invited to the party, I'd just have to have one of my own, was my reasoning.

I had no idea there were that many underwear models in the world as I watched them all traipse across the red carpet waving at their fans who stood behind velvet ropes. The hosts interviewed the most well known models and I was surprised to see that some of them were halfway intelligent. Well, that was rude of me. I couldn't let my dealings with one model in particular blemish my opinion of them all, I told myself.

Thirty minutes into the damned thing, I caught a glimpse of Jag shaking hands with the fans as he smiled at them, talking with a few. God, he was so handsome, looking gorgeous in his tux. There were a couple of models lined up in front of him who were with their boyfriends or spouses waiting to get some face time with the emcees, so I had to wait a bit to see his interview. As the second model walked onto the little stage where the interviews were taking place, I finally caught sight of Jag. Who was standing with the stunning Alessandra. Holding her hand. And smiling down at her as they chatted.

What?

Again, what?

My insides turned to ice as I sat up to watch what was happening right in front of my very eyes. I set the bottle of scotch on the coffee table and rubbed my eyes thinking I was probably drunk and just seeing things. But when I reopened them, nope, I'd seen everything as clear as day.

It was Jag and Alessandra's turn in the spotlight then.

The male host spoke into his microphone. "So, Jag, how does it feel to be The Sexiest Athlete of the Year?"

Jag had been awarded that title by another publication earlier in the month and we'd laughed about it because it seemed like the kudos just kept coming.

"Well, Mark, I guess it feels all right. I mean, it's better than being the ugliest athlete of the year, right?" Jag said with a chuckle.

Alessandra giggled at this and the emcee looked at her and asked, "Alessandra, how does it feel to be dating the Sexiest Athlete of the Year? I'm sure you're having to beat the women off of your beau, huh?"

She was still holding Jag's hand and brought her other hand up to caress his cheek as she smiled up at him then dropped it to rest against his chest. Oh. My. God.

"Oh, Mark, you know those women know better than to mess with my man," she said, still giggling. "He only has eyes for me, though." She looked up at Jag in adoration.

And Jag just smiled back at her. Um, what the fuck?

The host went on to ask Jag questions about how the season was going, but I didn't hear anything that was being said as I watched Alessandra doting on Jag, straightening his bowtie and sweeping that hunk of hair that always hung on his forehead out of the way. Argh! Before they left the stage, the announcer asked one more question.

"So, you guys planning on anything long-term with your relationship?"

I heard Jag utter an "Uh" but Alessandra jumped in before he could say anything. "Yes, I think we look perfect together, don't you agree? I'd bet we'd make some beautiful babies, wouldn't we, handsome?"

She looked up at Jag lovingly who nodded down at her.

Had the world gone fucking mad? Wow.

Before they left the interview area, Jag released her hand. About damned time! But then he put his hand at the small of her back as he led her away making her look up at him and smile, and that's when the first tear ran down my cheek.

My phone rang but I didn't answer. I just sat there stunned then proceeded to drink half of the bottle before passing out.

I woke up and grimaced at the pounding in my head. Stupid Macallans. I was still in my chair, so I sat up and grabbed my phone out of my lap seeing that it was almost two in the morning. I also saw that I had seven missed calls, three from Rebecca, one from Gwen, one from Robbie and two from Jag.

"Jag?" I called but got no answer. Where was he?

I got up and went into the bedroom, but he wasn't there. Must've been one hell of a party. I came back into the living room and turned off the TV as I checked my voicemail. Rebecca was pissed and wanted me to call her. Robbie was pissed and wanted to murder Jag. Gwen asked me to call her back if I needed her. And Jag had called to tell me that he'd be late and not to wait up for him.

I picked up the bottle of scotch and returned it to the cabinet when I heard someone talking loudly out in the hallway. I went to the door and looked through the peephole and saw Jag with his arm around Alessandra walking by. I unlocked the door and stepped out into the hall and screeched, "What the hell?"

Alessandra turned to me with a giggle as she wrapped her arms around Jag's neck. "What's the matter, little girlfriend? Jealous?" she said drunkenly.

If looks could kill, they'd have both dropped dead right about then. "Jag?" I said between clenched teeth.

"Hang on, El. Let me get her to her condo."

I gritted my teeth, taking a deep breath to keep myself from screaming then nodded and went back inside. Ten minutes later he came inside and we both stood just staring at each other.

"Look, El…"

"What the fuck *was* that, Jag?"

"She was drunk. I had to get her home."

My eyes bore into his. He knew what I was talking about and was avoiding it. "You know what I meant," I snapped.

His head went back, his hands went to his hips and he stood there studying the ceiling for a minute before looking back at me. "I'm tired of arguing about everything, El."

And that's when I lost it. "*You're* tired? What about me? I got to stay home tonight and watch *my* boyfriend act like he's another woman's boyfriend! What the fuck *was* that? I'm so humiliated! All my friends watched you be an asshole tonight!"

His jaw clenched and that's when he gave me the killing blow. "Maybe we should take a break."

"Wh-what?" I asked with a gasp, shocked that he'd say something like that.

He rubbed his eyes with the heels of his palms then looked at me and replied, "You're losing weight. You're an emotional mess. Maybe you should go home and be with people who can be there for you. I'm never around and I know I'm not good for you right now."

And that's when the anger surfaced and I went manic on him.

"Don't you dare stand there and pull some fucking *Twilight* vampire shit on me, Jagger Jensen! You're not good for me right now?" I huffed out a laugh. "Now that's just *classic*! And I'm only an emotional mess because you've made me that way with not putting your fucking foot down and standing up to that asshole of an agent you have!" I glared at him, knowing this was it. "You want me gone? Fine! I'm gone! So fuck you, Jag! Fuck you and fuck your goddamned 'Sexiest Athlete of the Year' bullshit! Fuck your career and fuck your fucking whore of a fucking fake girlfriend!"

I turned and ran into the bedroom, slamming and locking the door. I opened my phone and called Rebecca, and as I waited for her to answer, I heard Jag yell, "Fuck!" It was the word of the night. Then I heard the front door open and slam shut. I ended my call and raced out of the bedroom to the front door and out just in time to see Jag jogging to his car in the parking lot.

"Jag!" I called, not knowing what I'd even say if he came back, but he just turned and looked at me, the anguish in his eyes apparent, before getting into his Camaro, backing out and speeding off.

I flew home to Chicago the next afternoon. Jag didn't show up to say goodbye or see me off.

And I never went back.

Watch for *Finding Us* (True Love Trilogy, Book Two) coming in February 2014 and *Unbreakable Hearts* (CEP #2) coming in March 2014!

About the author:

Harper Bentley has taught high school English for 21 years. Although she's managed to maintain her sanity regardless of her career choice, jumping into the world of publishing her own books goes to show that she might be closer to the ledge than was previously thought.

After traveling the nation in her younger years as a military brat, having lived in Alaska, Washington State and California, she now resides in Oklahoma with her teenage daughter, two dogs and one cat, happily writing stories that she hopes her readers will enjoy.

You can contact her at HarperBentleyWrites@gmail.com, at http://harperbentleywrites.com/, on Facebook or follow her on Twitter @HarperBentley

Made in the USA
Charleston, SC
26 February 2014